SCAM AND EGGS

SCAM AND EGGS

Stories by

Janet Dawson

Five Star • Waterville, Maine

Five Star First Edition Mystery Series.
First Printing

Published in 2002 in conjunction with Tekno Books and
Ed Gorman.

Set in 11 pt. Plantin.

Printed in the United States on permanent paper.

Library of Congress Cataloging-in-Publication Data

Dawson, Janet.
    Scam and eggs : stories / by Janet Dawson.
        p. cm.—(Five Star first edition mystery series.)
    Contents: Scam and eggs—Witchcraft—Little red
Corvette—Voice mail—Blue eyes—Mrs. Lincoln's
dilemma—Pack rat—By the book—What the cat dragged in
—Invisible time.
    ISBN 0-7862-4838-6 (hc : alk. paper)
    1. Detective and mystery stories, American. I. Title.
II. Series.
PS3554.A949 S38 2002
813'.54—dc21   2002029968

To my parents,
Don and Thelma Dawson

Table of Contents

Introduction

Back when I was in junior high school, I read a book by Hildegarde Dolson, called *We Shook the Family Tree*. I enjoyed the author's amusing tales of growing up in a small Pennsylvania town in the early part of the twentieth century, but what I remember most about Dolson's memoir was her aspiration to be a writer. I, too, longed to be a writer, so I understood. At the end of the book Dolson described how, after much rejection, she finally sold her first short story to *The New Yorker*, thus launching her career as a published writer.

I was impressed. I thought, if Hildegarde can do it, so can I.

Until that time, my only notable efforts at writing, outside of school work, were an illustrated story penned in the fifth grade—a mystery, naturally—and a play I'd written in the sixth grade. The play had so impressed my teacher that my class performed the work for the first-graders.

So I began writing short stories and sending them out to magazines, just the way it says you're supposed to in all those articles I read in *Writer's Digest* and *The Writer*. I got the results you would expect—rejection slips. But I looked at them in a positive light. I was the only eighth-grader in my school with a sheaf of my very own rejection slips—from some highly-regarded magazines, too.

In high school I channeled my urge to write into articles for the student newspaper and a short story or two for English class. In college, my poetry and a short story or two were published in the college literary magazine. Then as college segued into real life, I became a small-town newspaper reporter who wrote about city council meetings, then later a Navy journalist who wrote about training schools.

Still, fiction beckoned. I started a short story that got longer and longer, and ultimately grew into a novel that didn't sell. I found that I preferred the larger, more complex framework of the novel. There was more room to tell the story, more space for digression. I began writing another novel that didn't sell, then finally a third novel that became *Kindred Crimes*, the first book in my series featuring Oakland private investigator Jeri Howard.

I didn't write short stories any more, not for a long time. Then one day, after I'd finally achieved my goal—a published novel—I got an invitation from Marilyn Wallace to contribute a short story to the *Sisters in Crime* anthology she was then editing. I said yes. My focus shifted, if only temporarily, from the novel back to the short story.

Telling a tale completely and succinctly, in the spare and stripped-down framework of the short story, presents a different set of challenges from the novel, where the writer has more time and space in which to work. But these stories have provided me with a welcome opportunity to stretch, to use different characters and different time periods, to explore ideas that are intriguing but perhaps not large enough to contain a novel.

My short stories begin with an idea or an image, frequently from real life. Then fiction takes over and the story grows. Here, then, are the stories, and the seeds that helped them germinate and grow.

"Scam and Eggs" is a new story, but one with ties to the Jeri Howard series. Jeri's back story in Kindred Crimes *includes the information that she was a legal secretary and paralegal before becoming a private investigator in a firm headed by the dapper Errol Seville. But Errol and his wife Minna have retired to Carmel, so Jeri has gone out on her own. Errol and Minna put in appearances in two later Jeri Howard novels,* Don't Turn Your Back on the Ocean *and* A Credible Threat. *Here they solve a mystery of their own, inspired by my visit to a museum exhibit featuring one of the fabulous Fabergé Easter eggs created for the Czar's family of Russia.*

Scam and Eggs

"The Rodrigos have a Fabergé egg," Minna Seville said.

Errol Seville smiled. "How very ostentatious of them."

The retired private investigator and his wife stood on the patio behind an art gallery on Dolores Avenue in Carmel-by-the-Sea, sipping mediocre champagne and nibbling on hors d'oeuvres as they watched the people around them. It was a Saturday in April, almost the dinner hour, and to the west, the sun was beginning its afternoon descent toward the turquoise waters of Carmel Bay.

"I'm impressed, even if you aren't," Minna retorted. "Those eggs are priceless, because there are so few of them. Fabergé made fifty-six eggs for the Russian royal family. Only forty-four of them survive, in museums or private collections. I saw several of them, a few years ago at that exhibit up in San Francisco. The eggs are incredible—detailed work, decorated with jewels, and they all have tiny little surprises inside. It must be a coup for a dealer or a collector to find one."

"I didn't say I wasn't impressed. Merely curious. When did Rodrigo acquire this trinket?" Errol's eyes narrowed as he looked through the open doorway leading into the gallery. "He didn't have it when I investigated his insurance claim after that so-called robbery."

That had been several years ago, before Errol's age, combined with his last heart attack, forced the investigator to close the Seville Agency. He and Minna had sold their house in Oakland and headed south, to the retirement home they'd

purchased long before housing prices on the Monterey penin-
sula had moved from merely pricey to completely insane.

Back then, Paul Rodrigo had owned a gallery called Xian
on San Francisco's Union Street, specializing in Asian art
and antiques. One day Rodrigo had called the police to report
a robbery. He said he'd arrived at his gallery that morning to
discover a door forced open at the back of the gallery and the
alarm system turned off. Several display cases had been
smashed and a number of valuable, and heavily insured,
objects had been taken. All of the missing items—ivory
netsukes, jade jewelry, old cloisonné ornaments—were small,
easily disposed of, and difficult to trace. None had ever been
recovered.

The Seville Agency had been hired by the insurance company to investigate Rodrigo's expensive claim, to see if it was
valid. As far as Errol was concerned, there were some things
about Rodrigo's statement to the police that didn't hold
water. The detective had also discovered that the gallery
owner was sometimes less than fastidious about the prove-
nance of some of the items he sold.

Rodrigo and his assistant, Tina Leong, both swore they'd
set the alarm system before leaving the night before. If that
was true, someone had turned off the alarm, which should
have sounded the moment the door opened. The company
that made the system hadn't found anything wrong with it, so
a malfunction didn't seem likely.

The other possibility was that someone had obtained the
alarm system code. But Tina Leong, who'd worked for
Rodrigo about a year, was innocent of any wrongdoing, as
Errol ultimately determined. That left Rodrigo. Errol suspected from the start that the gallery owner had engineered
the robbery, disposed of the missing items himself, and collected the insurance money to boot. The investigator was

even more convinced after he learned that Rodrigo had owned a gallery in New Orleans before he moved to San Francisco, and that Rodrigo's gallery there had experienced a similar robbery with a similar result.

But Errol hadn't been able to confirm his suspicions about Rodrigo's culpability, so the gallery owner had collected the large insurance settlement. Not long afterward, Rodrigo had given up his lease on the Union Street space, sold his stock, and left the city. Errol checked to see where Rodrigo had gone, and discovered that the object of his scrutiny had surfaced in Scottsdale, just outside Phoenix. He'd opened another gallery, this one specializing in Southwestern art. Errol wondered how long it would be before the Scottsdale police were called to the scene of yet another gallery theft. But after Rodrigo's departure from San Francisco, and Errol Seville's radar screen, other cases and other life events intervened. Errol hadn't given the gallery owner or their previous encounter any thought for years—until last Wednesday.

Errol had been out for his daily constitutional, which included coffee with friends at a local beanery, then a walk to the Carmel village post office at Fifth and Dolores. After collecting the mail from the Sevilles' post office box, he'd set out in the direction of home. Then he stopped, his eye caught by a sign in the window of a retail building in the block between Fifth and Sixth. The building was redwood, two stories high, with two storefronts on the sidewalk and offices on the second floor. A signboard listed the upstairs tenants as a lawyer and an accountant. One of the storefronts was occupied by a jewelry store. The other had until recently been leased to an upscale women's clothing boutique. Now another business was moving into this particular space. Large letters at the top of a pasteboard sign in the window read, "Opening soon, Livadia."

15

So what the hell was Livadia? Errol peered in the window and saw empty glass display cases arrayed around the room. Then he stepped back and squinted at the sign through the lower half of his bifocals. The smaller print told him that Livadia was a gallery featuring European art and antiques. It was to open in three days, on Saturday, and there would be a champagne reception to celebrate that fact, from five to seven that evening.

Another gallery, Errol told himself. Just what Carmel needs.

He was about to step away and continue his walk home, when he saw movement at the back of the gallery, where another door led past an office to the back of the building. A man and a woman stood in the doorway, talking. Then the woman moved out of view and he got a good look at the man. The face was familiar. Where had he seen that face before? He mentally flipped through the faces and the cases he'd worked on while he was in the private investigating business. It was a long list, so it took a moment for him to put a name with this particular face.

By God, he chuckled as the penny dropped into the slot. Paul Rodrigo.

"Once a private eye, always a private eye," Minna said, when her husband came home to tell her that they'd be attending the gallery opening on Saturday. "I suppose you're going to be doing surveillance."

"Once a crook, always a crook," Errol told her. "This is the fourth gallery this guy has had in ten years, and he's had robberies followed by big insurance claims at two of them. And at the third, I'm willing to bet. Mark my words, he's going to try it again. I'm going to find out everything I can about this new gallery. I want you to nose around, too."

"What am I, your operative?" Minna gave her husband a

fond look as she shooed their big black-and-white cat Stinkpot off the kitchen counter. The fat feline knew he wasn't supposed to be up there, but he hadn't been able to resist batting at the blossoms on the dendrobium orchid Minna was watering in the sink.

"One of my best," Errol said, bending down to nuzzle Minna's cheek. "Besides, you know everything that goes on in Carmel village. So get out there and do your stuff. Report back when you've got something."

Stinkpot was ignoring Minna, so she picked him up and deposited him on the floor. He huffed at her and stalked off in the direction of the living room. "And what will you be doing, staking out the gallery?"

"Got to do some legwork first," Errol said.

The legwork involved a visit to the county courthouse branch in Monterey. Errol spent a couple of hours looking at the new business licenses and the real estate transactions, confirming that Paul Rodrigo, late of Scottsdale, had indeed moved to Carmel to open the gallery called Livadia. He'd also gotten married along the way. The other name on the deed of an expensive house in Carmel Highlands was Mercedes Rodrigo.

When he got back home, Errol went to the kitchen for a glass of iced tea, then reached for the kitchen telephone, a cordless. He stepped over Stinkpot, who was sprawled out in the kitchen traffic pattern because that's where the sun was, and went out to the back yard, where Minna was pulling weeds in one of the flower beds. Errol punched in the number of one of his former operatives who now worked as a sole proprietor. The phone rang twice, then a voice answered. "Howard Investigations."

"I need you to check on something, and someone," Errol said.

"You've got a computer," Jeri Howard said. "You could do that yourself."

"I'm supposed to be retired, as Minna keeps reminding me. Besides, I thought you might enjoy this one. Remember Paul Rodrigo?"

"Vaguely. Insurance claim, wasn't it?" There was a pause on the other end of the phone, as though Jeri was sifting through her memories of cases gone by. "Rodrigo. Robbery claim. Had a gallery on Union Street, didn't he? And you thought he robbed the place himself."

"Bingo," Errol said. "And when we looked into it, we found out that before he came to San Francisco, he'd had a gallery on Magazine Street in New Orleans. Which had a similar robbery and a similar large insurance claim. But we couldn't prove he was scamming and the insurance company paid the claim on the Union Street robbery. Not long after, Rodrigo departed foggy Frisco for sunny Scottsdale. Now he's about to open yet another gallery in Carmel."

"And you want me to find out if he had any robberies or insurance claims in Scottsdale," Jeri said. "And a little background check while I'm at it. That's easy enough to do. What are you going to do on your end?"

"I've already been to the courthouse," he told her. "He's got a business license for this new gallery. It's called Livadia. He's selling European stuff this time. And he bought an overpriced shack in Carmel Highlands. By the way, he's got something now that he didn't have before. A wife. Her name's Mercedes."

"She sounds very upscale," Jeri said. "What does she look like?"

"Haven't gotten a look at her yet, but I'm sure I will on Saturday. He's having an opening. Minna and I will be there to case him, her and the joint."

"And not coincidentally suck up some free booze and munchies," Jeri added.

Errol laughed. "You know me well. Run a backgrounder on Mrs. Rodrigo while you're at it. Ta, Jeri. I'll give Stinkpot a scratch behind the ears in your name."

"You'll be lucky if you don't get a scratch on the hand if you do anything to that cat in my name," Jeri said darkly. "Stinkpot hates me."

"Not really. He's just an acquired taste."

Jeri laughed. "Or vice versa. He hasn't acquired a taste for me yet. Unless it's to bite me with his fangs."

The cat in question floated from the kitchen floor to the counter as Errol hung up the phone, perhaps lured by the sound of his name and the possibility that a cat treat might be in the offing. Errol scratched Stinkpot behind the ears and got swatted with a paw for his efforts.

When Saturday rolled around, Errol and Minna had arrived at the gallery opening around five-thirty. The gallery was full of people, many of them crowding around a table full of hors d'oeuvres. A white-coated man at another table at the back dispensed champagne and sparkling water. Just inside the entrance, Errol stopped and looked around, noting the layout of the place. The front door was bracketed by plate glass windows, and opposite that, at the back of the gallery, another door led out to a patio behind the retail complex. On the wall to his right and about ten feet ahead of him was a small counter. A shelf in back of this held a small CD player with speakers, playing classical music. Mahler, Errol thought, listening for a moment.

Errol looked around for Rodrigo and spotted him in the far corner, talking with several of his guests. The gallery owner hadn't changed much in the years since Errol had seen him. He was in his mid-fifties now, of medium height, a bit stocky around the middle, but he looked fit. His silver hair was neatly trimmed and set off his tennis court tan.

Errol took Minna's arm. He'd noticed a door just beyond the counter that was slightly ajar. It just begged for a look to see what was behind it. When he pushed the door open, he saw that it led to a short hallway. A door on the right was closed. When Errol tried to turn the knob, he found that the door was locked. Must be the gallery's office, he said to himself. To the left, down the hall, was a utilitarian room with boxes and packing material. A blue cotton smock hung from a hook on the door. Between the office and the stockroom was a small bathroom with a toilet, sink, and a small rattan shelf unit holding supplies.

"You're so nosy." Minna tugged on Errol's sleeve.

Errol was unrepentant. "It's my calling."

"Would you at least get me some champagne before you search the joint? Besides, it's not like you to be so obvious."

"I'm not being obvious," Errol said. "If anyone asks, I'm looking for the john."

He took Minna's hand and they stepped back into the gallery. Rodrigo was still holding court over in the corner. Errol acquired a plate and snagged some of the hors d'oeuvres, then he and Minna took a couple of glasses of champagne outside onto the patio, where it was cooler and a little quieter. However, the free booze and munchies were not up to Minna's exacting standards.

"I don't know where he got this champagne," she said after a few sips, "but it's utter swill. And this crab puff is mostly puff." She wrapped the rest of the offending morsel in a cocktail napkin and deposited it and her half-full glass on a nearby tray.

"Have to agree with you there." Errol set his glass and the plate on the tray.

"What did Jeri have to say about Rodrigo's gallery in Scottsdale?"

"As I suspected," Errol said. "Rodrigo reported a robbery about a year ago. Same MO as the place on Union Street. The missing items included a lot of extremely portable Navajo turquoise and silver jewelry, Zuni fetishes, and Pueblo pottery—none of which were ever recovered. The insurance company paid out a very large sum of money for that purported loss. Money which no doubt went into this latest gallery and the fancy house in the Highlands that he's sharing with the new Mrs. Rodrigo."

"It's a huge house, too," Minna said. "I talked with the real estate agent. It was the first place the Rodrigos looked at. They made an offer right away, several thousand bucks above the asking price."

"So they really must have wanted it," Errol said. "Or they were in a hurry to get established here, and didn't want to waste more time looking. Mercedes is thirty-six, which makes her twenty years younger than her husband. Rodrigo will be fifty-seven later this year. She was born in San Bernardino and she's been profitably divorced from a dentist in La Jolla for seven years. Since then she's moved around quite a bit. Jeri found former addresses for her in Los Angeles, Chicago, and New York City. She and Rodrigo got married thirteen months ago, in Scottsdale. So tell me, my love. What does the Carmel rumor mill say about Mercedes?"

"I did you one better than the Carmel rumor mill. I actually talked with her," Minna said. "A couple of days ago when I 'accidentally' ran into her at the grocery store. Since she's new to the area she seemed eager to make a connection. At first I thought she was playing the role of the dumb brunette. But I think she's smarter than she lets on. Once I got her going she was quite informative. They've been in the house about six weeks. They were living at the Carmel Highlands Inn until they could move in, and going back and forth to Scottsdale a lot. She says she met Rodrigo about eighteen months ago, at an auction house in New York City. That's where he bought the Fabergé egg. Romance ensued, followed by whirlwind courtship and marriage. Then, presumably, connubial bliss in Scottsdale and now Carmel."

"Rodrigo isn't the connubial bliss type," Errol said. "He's more the arm candy type. At least that was the case when he lived in San Francisco. He likes to acquire pretty things. Mercedes is just his most recent acquisition. Like the egg. Let's have a look at this trinket."

"The wife or the egg?" Minna asked.

When they reentered the crowded gallery, Rodrigo was near the front door. Standing next to him was a sleek brunette, nearly as tall as he was. She wore a yellow silk dress with long flowing sleeves and a plunging neckline that showed off a heavy gold necklace and an attractive bosom. The skirt had an uneven hem and slits in the sides, revealing an admirable pair of legs.

Minna caught Errol's appreciative stare and dug an elbow into her husband's side. "Just which trinket did you have in mind? You're too old for her, my love."

"He's too old for her," Errol said in his own defense.

Rodrigo looked up and Errol did a quick about-face. He didn't want the gallery owner to see him, at least not yet. As he looked over Minna's head, toward the back of the gallery, his gaze fell on another familiar face. "Well, well, well, this is like old home week."

Minna turned around for a better look. "The man in gray? Who is he?"

"His name is Barry Kezer," Errol said. "And he's a thief."

The dark-haired man wore gray slacks and a gray silk shirt,

and he was a little older, a little grayer than he'd been the last time Errol had seen him. Kezer specialized in jewelry. When he wasn't hitting jewelry stores, like the one right next door, Kezer's MO was to prowl events like this—gallery openings, symphony galas, fundraisers and banquets—looking for baubles and relieving them from their owners with a touch as smooth as the silk shirt he was wearing today. He'd worked San Francisco for a few years until things got too hot for him in the city by the bay. So he'd departed, for the Big Apple, Errol thought, although he'd heard that Kezer had also been spotted in Los Angeles, San Diego and points in between.

Kezer was casing the joint, his eyes moving restlessly. He wasn't eating or drinking, Errol noticed. The thief was leaving his hands free because he was looking for a easy pickings, a chance to score here among the well-decorated citizens of Carmel. And there were plenty of pickings. As Errol scanned the room, he noted trinkets of every size and description, expensive jewelry on women's necks, arms and fingers.

Or maybe Kezer was after a bigger score. Like the Fabergé egg Rodrigo had here in the gallery. It wouldn't be the first time the thief had branched out.

There was a flurry of movement and sound at the gallery's front door. "Someone's making an entrance," Minna said. "Oh, it's Adam Trask, that movie director who just bought a big house out near Pebble Beach."

"Never heard of him," Errol said.

"That's because you don't watch any movies except the ones on Turner Classics."

"That's because they don't make movies like those any more. You can have new Hollywood. I prefer the old."

"Well, I don't think Trask claims to be the next Billy Wilder."

"I should hope not." Errol narrowed his eyes, focusing on

the athletic-looking, sandy-haired man in khakis who had stuck his sunglasses in the V-neck of his black knit shirt.

"But Trask does make movies," Minna said. "Those action adventure things with lots of car chases and explosions, starring actors we never heard of."

"Thank God for cable," Errol said. "Does this Trask fellow collect art? He must have some interest in it, since he's at a gallery opening on a Saturday evening. He certainly didn't come for the food or booze."

Minna shrugged. "I don't know. I heard that he did buy two rather large oil paintings from a gallery over on Ocean Avenue. Either he likes art, or he just has a big house to decorate."

Errol watched as Trask glad-handed several people at the front of the gallery, then moved through the crowd toward Rodrigo. The gallery owner shook the director's hand and then introduced him to Mercedes, who had appeared at his side. Mercedes shook Trask's hand, then moved away, in the direction of the white-coated man who was still pouring the mediocre champagne. Kezer was there, too, hovering in the doorway that led out to the patio. Errol saw the jewel thief give Mercedes the once-over. Was he checking out her voluptuous figure, or the gold necklace that encircled her neck?

Errol and Minna moved across the gallery. They passed behind Trask and Rodrigo, who were standing in the middle of the room, near a display case. Errol's ears pricked as he heard Trask mutter a figure, a large sum. Rodrigo shook his head.

"Damn it," Trask said. "I want it and I'm willing to pay for it. How can I change your mind? What can I do or say?"

"Nothing," Rodrigo said. "I told you, it's not for sale, to you or anyone else. Now if you'll excuse me."

The gallery owner turned and stopped, face to face with

24

the Sevilles. Errol's mouth curved into his foxy, cat-that-ate-the-canary smile, but he didn't say anything. He knew the gallery owner recognized him. Rodrigo's face whitened under his tan, and his mouth tightened into a tense line. He stepped away, walking toward the front of the gallery.

"He knew you," Minna said.

"I doubt he'd forget me," Errol said. "I held up payment of his insurance claim for months."

The soothing classical piece on the CD player had been replaced by something loud and annoying, with lots of brass and crashing cymbals. Wagner. Errol hated Wagner.

"Hello. It's nice to see you again." Mercedes Rodrigo had strolled over to greet them. Her sleeves were so long they partly obscured her hands, one of which was wrapped around the stem of the champagne glass she carried. Errol couldn't tell from the smile on the younger woman's face whether she remembered Minna from their earlier encounter, or whether she was just being polite. "What do you think of our gallery?"

"It's lovely," Minna said. "I was just telling my husband what you told me the other day in the grocery store, about that Fabergé egg. I wondered if we could just take a peek. I've never seen one outside of a museum."

Mercedes tilted her head to one side, overplaying it a bit as she considered Minna's request. "Well, I guess there wouldn't be any harm in one little peek," she said, with a breathy little giggle.

She glanced over her shoulder, as though looking to see where her husband was, then she beckoned Errol and Minna to follow her. She set her champagne glass on the end of the counter, then the three of them went through the door that led to the short hallway. It was empty. Mercedes tucked her hand into a pocket hidden at the waist of her of her yellow silk dress and drew out a brass key. She unlocked the door and opened it. "It's on the top shelf of that glass case."

Errol quickly surveyed the inner sanctum. The office had white walls and no windows. The furnishings were what one would expect to see in an office—desk, computer stand, lateral filing cabinets, shelves. All the pieces except the office chair behind the desk were made of laminated particle board, the cheap stuff that comes unassembled. Rodrigo must have put his money into the public portion of the gallery, where the display cases and counters were highly-polished wood, Errol thought, and decided to cut corners in the part of the gallery that no one would see. Rodrigo had also put his money into his stock, the objets d'art that he planned to sell. Some of them were no doubt stored in the large safe in the corner nearest the door. And others were displayed in the sturdy-looking case next to it. The cabinet was constructed of metal and glass, about four feet high, two feet wide and perhaps fifteen inches deep. It had a keyed padlock on the door. Inside were four glass shelves, lighted to show the objects inside.

Errol stepped closer to examine the contents. The bottom three shelves held a jeweled mace, a heavy gold collar that looked medieval, and a collection of enamel and porcelain boxes that glittered with gemstones. The top shelf held only the Fabergé.

The egg was about four inches high, five if Errol counted the gold stand on which it rested. The egg's exterior was pale turquoise enamel, the top looking a bit like one of those Russian onion domes, embellished with tiny pearls. On the bottom of the egg, diamonds, rubies, sapphires and emeralds flashed their fire. The egg had been opened to reveal the surprise Fabergé had placed inside, in this instance a little gazebo made of gold, surrounded by tiny flowers made of precious stones.

"I'm impressed," Errol confessed. "It's exquisite."

"Isn't it just fabulous?" Mercedes said, her voice almost reverent. "When I saw it in that auction house in New York City, I was just bowled over."

Errol looked sideways at her. Had Mercedes decided to marry Rodrigo when he acquired the Fabergé egg? No doubt Minna would accuse him of being cynical. But when he glanced at his wife, he knew from the twinkle in her eyes that she was thinking the same thing. He looked at the egg again, wondering about its value and the amount of insurance coverage Rodrigo had on it, because he was sure Rodrigo was going to try his scam again. Sooner or later there would be a robbery at this gallery and the Fabergé egg would go missing.

"We should probably join the others," Mercedes said.

"Of course." Errol straightened, then stopped, bemused by the objects he saw on the desk and the nearby shelves. Not objets d'art, but a collection of a more plebeian nature. "What's this?" He walked closer to examine the objects. Snow globes, sometimes called water globes. There were dozens of them, some large and elaborate, the kind with music boxes in the base. Others were small, cheap souvenirs readily available in tourist shops all over the world. All of them had some sort of scene inside, with fake snow or glitter that swirled through the liquid inside when the globe was shaken.

"You've caught me," Mercedes said with a self-deprecating giggle. "I collect snow globes. The tackier, the better."

Errol picked up one of the snow globes, this one sitting on the desk. It was large and quite heavy, resting on a thick, square base. Inside the globe was a New York City skyline with the Empire State Building amid the gray skyscrapers and the Statue of Liberty, painted gold. The legend "I Love New York" was painted in red letters on each of the four sides of the base. He shook it vigorously and watched the white flecks suspended in the clear liquid swirl around Lady Liberty. This one had a music box in the base. He wound the key on the bottom and listened as the first few bars of "New York, New York" tinkled over and over again.

Mercedes shrugged. "I know, it's silly. But I love them. I buy them wherever I go. Airport shops, souvenir stands. My friends keep trying to improve my taste, so they buy me the more expensive kind with music boxes, like the one you're holding. But I just can't resist ticky-tacky. Like this one." She picked up another globe, the cheap touristy kind, and shook it. This globe was larger than a softball, and it had gold flecks in pale blue liquid. The plastic scene inside showed a San Francisco landscape complete with a bright orange Golden Gate Bridge, red cable cars climbing a large hill decorated with blue and green buildings, and a bright yellow Coit Tower.

"Well, thank you for letting us look at the egg," Errol said, putting the New York City globe back on the desk. "We should rejoin the others before we're missed."

"You're right," Mercedes said. She set the San Francisco globe on the desk and reached into her pocket for the door key. They left the office and Mercedes locked the door behind them. Once they were back out in the gallery, Mercedes headed for the front of the gallery, where Rodrigo stood. Errol leaned over to Minna. "Interesting that she's got those things displayed here. I would think she'd keep them at home."

"They're in the loo, too," Minna said. "I noticed when I was in there earlier. The Alamo, Disneyland and Mount Rushmore are lined up on the rattan shelf next to the sink."

"Besides," Errol said thoughtfully, "my impression from past encounters with Rodrigo is that he's quite a snob where

art is concerned. Snow globes in the same room as his
Fabergé egg?"

"Maybe it's love," Minna said.

"I doubt it."

Wagner was still crashing out of the CD player in the gallery. It was nearly seven, and Errol thought by now that
people would have been leaving the gallery opening. The
table with the hors d'oeuvres looked picked over, and the
champagne supply appeared to be dwindling. Instead, the
party seems to be ratcheting up, the noise level increasing.
Errol and Minna were waylaid by some neighbors, a retired
couple who lived on the same street as the Sevilles. A few
minutes into the conversation, Errol looked around for Barry
Kezer and didn't see him. Then he spotted the jewel thief
coming through the door that led back to the office and bathroom. Perhaps he'd been using the facilities—or checking out
the office door that Mercedes had relocked.

Kezer walked toward the table where the champagne was
being poured. He loitered there for a moment or two, not
asking for a glass, his eyes flicking over the people around
him. Errol tried to figure out which of the nearby bejeweled
women Kezer was targeting. That blonde in the red dress,
smoothing back her hair with her right hand—was that big
diamond cocktail ring easy to slip off her finger? The brunette
in the beige linen slacks and blouse—was the catch loose on
that sapphire necklace she wore?

Now, as Errol watched, Kezer turned, as though to walk
away from the drinks table. He bumped into the woman in
the red dress, throwing her off-balance. Momentum propelled the woman forward, into the table that held the champagne glasses. The table wobbled, then tipped. Screams min-
gled with the tinkle of breaking glass, and everyone rushed
over to see what was happening. Errol wasn't sure when

Kezer had taken the ring. It could have been as he bumped her or when his hands joined the others that helped steady her. All the detective knew was when the woman brushed and straightened her red dress, the big diamond sparkler was gone.

Kezer headed for the front door, walking slowly but directly. Errol stepped in front of him and clamped a hand around the jewel thief's forearm. "Hello, Barry," he said in a low tone. "What have you got in your pocket? Besides the ring. Looks like there were a lot of things to choose from this afternoon."

Kezer stared hard at him, as though trying to place a name with the face. "I don't know what you're talking about."

"Of course you do," Errol said. "I saw you pull the same stunt at the Symphony Gala in San Francisco a few years ago. I caught you then, too."

Minna already had the cell phone out of her purse and her fingers hovered over the keypad. "Shall I?"

"Seville! Damn it." Kezer remembered him now. The thief tried to pull his arm away but Errol held tight. "Let go of me, old man, or I'll knock you down." He glanced over Errol's shoulder, in the direction of the front door, as though gauging his chances of getting through it.

The woman in red had discovered that her ring was missing and was being quite vocal about it. Kezer was a lot younger and stronger than Errol was, so the detective looked around for some help. The nearest warm body was Adam Trask. The director had just come through the doorway leading back to the bathroom, a splotch of water visible on his khaki slacks. "I believe this man took the lady's ring," Errol told Trask. "I'd appreciate it if you'd hang onto him for a moment while we call the police."

"Sure thing," Trask said. He grabbed Kezer enthusiastically as the jewel thief struggled.

Mercedes Rodrigo came up from behind Errol, just as Minna started to punch numbers into the cell phone. "Let's take this into the office," she said, her voice tense, "where it's a little less public. I'm sure Paul . . . Say, where is Paul?"

She looked around and so did Errol, but the gallery owner was nowhere in sight.

"I was talking with him on the patio a little while ago," Trask said. "But he came back in here."

"I think I saw him out on the front sidewalk," another woman said. "With someone who was leaving. I'll go get him."

"Please do," Mercedes said. She led the way into the back hallway, pulling the office key from her pocket as she moved. She reached for the knob and stuck the key into the lock. The knob moved under her hand. "It's unlocked. He must be in the office. Paul?"

She pushed the door open, then stopped, staring inside. Then she screamed.

Errol quickly stepped past the others and into the office. Paul Rodrigo lay face-down on the floor in front of his desk, his feet toward the door. His head and one of the larger snow globes—the New York City music box that Errol had seen earlier—lay just a few inches from the display case. The back of Rodrigo's head and the base of the snow globe were smeared and wet with blood. The case was open. Errol looked at the top shelf. The Fabergé egg was gone.

"I want to report a murder," Minna said into the cell phone. She gave the dispatcher the address and some details, then she disconnected and slipped the phone back into her purse. "They're on their way." It wouldn't take them long to get here. The Carmel Police Department was at Fourth and Junipero, only a few blocks away from the gallery.

Mercedes looked as though she was about to collapse. Errol took her arm and escorted her out to the gallery, away from the crime scene. His commanding voice cut through the chatter. "Nobody leaves. There's been a crime. The police are on their way. Shut the front door. Turn off that CD player. And somebody get Mrs. Rodrigo a chair."

The annoying Wagner piece halted abruptly as someone hit a button on top of the player. Errol's neighbor moved quickly to stand in front of the gallery entrance. A chair appeared, dragged in from the patio, and Mercedes sank into it. Tears streamed down her face and she wiped them away with both hands, the sleeves of her yellow silk dress absorbing the moisture. She'd stain the fabric, Errol thought. She already had, sometime during this afternoon's party. The yellow fabric was discolored, with a faint green tinge at the edges of both sleeves.

"Some water," Minna told Errol.

Errol turned and picked up an empty wine glass someone had left on the counter. He stepped across the hallway to the small bathroom and reached for the faucet, preparing to rinse out the glass and fill it with water. Then he stopped and peered at the sink trap. A half-empty bottle of sparkling water had been left on the rattan shelf next to the sink, amid the cheap plastic snow globes. He jumped up and down a couple of times. Minna, who had followed him into the hallway, looked at him as though he'd lost his mind. He smiled at her and handed her the wine glass. Then he picked up the bottle of sparkling water and carried it back to Mercedes. She was gulping the water down when the Carmel police cruiser pulled up outside.

It took some time for the authorities to process the crime scene and remove the body. Finally the investigating officer, Sergeant Mike Withers, began interviewing witnesses.

"When was the last time you saw your husband?" he asked Mercedes.

"Twenty, maybe thirty minutes before we found . . ." Mercedes shuddered. "He was out on the patio behind the gallery. He was talking with Mr. Trask. They were arguing."

The director looked indignant. "We were not arguing. We were having a conversation."

"Were you disagreeing about something?" Sergeant Withers asked.

"Well . . ." Trask hesitated.

"He wanted the egg. And Paul didn't want to sell it to him. Trask kept pressuring Paul. He was very insistent. Belligerent about it, when Paul said no."

"Now wait a minute," Trask said. "Sure I wanted that egg. Who wouldn't? Yes, I offered to buy it. Several times. And he turned me down several times. That doesn't mean I killed him."

Withers rubbed his chin. "What were you talking about out on the patio?"

"I made him a final offer for the egg. But he wouldn't sell. I told him fine, I wouldn't bring it up again. That's all."

"You were coming out of the office right before we found the body," Mercedes said.

"I'd been to the john," Trask said. "I had to take a leak."

Errol nodded. "I saw Trask coming through the door that led to the hallway. He had a damp spot on his trousers. I assumed he'd used the bathroom."

"He could have been washing blood off his pants," Mercedes said.

Errol and Withers traded looks over her head. Whoever had killed Rodrigo had been careful not to get blood on his—or her—clothing. The killer had worn the blue smock Errol had seen earlier, hanging on the door of the stockroom. The

33

crime scene techs had found the bloodstained garment wadded into a ball and buried under some papers in the wastebasket in the corner of the office.

"This is ridiculous," Trask protested. He pointed a thumb at Barry Kezer, now in the custody of the police. "What about light fingers there? He was coming out of the can as I went back there."

Kezer was shaking his head. He'd had the diamond ring in his pockets when the cops had searched him, as well as an emerald brooch and a pearl necklace. But they didn't find the Fabergé egg. Errol was sure the egg had been concealed somewhere in the gallery.

"I steal jewels," Kezer said. "Nice and portable, easy to fence. That egg's too rich for my blood. Besides, I never went near that office. You can't prove that I did."

Errol caught Sergeant Withers's eye. The detective excused himself and stepped over to the counter. "I don't think either man took the egg," Errol said. "Or killed Rodrigo."

"So what happened?" Withers asked Errol.

"Indulge me for a moment," Errol said. He walked into the office and stared at the desk, then moved his eyes up to the shelves. Then he jumped up and down a few times, the way he had earlier in the bathroom. Then he turned to Withers with a smile. "I think I can tell you who killed Paul Rodrigo. And where to find that Fabergé egg."

It was late by the time Errol and Minna Seville returned home. Errol poured each of them a glass of wine and they sat out on their patio, watching Stinkpot chase moths.

"How did you know Kezer was involved in stealing the egg?" Minna asked

"Now that was a hunch," Errol admitted. "But he deliberately made that woman in the red dress stumble into the drinks table. I thought he'd done it so he could steal her ring. But then it occurred to me that he might have done it to create a diversion, so his accomplice could steal the egg. When I caught him after he stole the ring, he looked over my shoulder. At the time, I thought he was looking at the front door. But he was probably looking at his accomplice, looking for help."

"And that was when Mercedes came up behind you and suggested going into the office."

"Where we could all conveniently find Rodrigo's body," Errol said.

"What made you suspect Mercedes?" Minna asked. "I know she had the key to the office, so it was safe to assume that she also had a key to the display case. But something else must have tipped you off."

"It was the stain on her sleeve," Errol said. "She wore the smock to make sure she didn't get blood on her dress when she bludgeoned her husband with the New York City snow globe, the one with the corners on the heavy base."

Minna nodded. "Which she had left on the desk when we were in the office earlier, easy for her to reach."

"Right. Mercedes and Kezer had been planning to steal the egg during the gallery opening and retrieve it later. I don't know when killing Rodrigo entered the picture. But it was the gold flecks in the sink trap that tipped me off. Mercedes got her sleeves wet when she emptied the liquid from one of the snow globes into the bathroom sink. The glitter in the liquid got stuck in the trap. It would have been easy for her to pry open any one of those cheap plastic snow globes. But most of them were too small to hide the Fabergé egg inside after she'd taken it out of the display case."

"So why were you jumping up and down in the bathroom and the office?"

Errol laughed. "I jumped to see if the liquid inside those globes in the bathroom moved. It did. So I figured it must have been one of the globes in the office. This time when I jumped up and down, the liquid in all of them moved. Except one. The San Francisco globe with the cable car climbing the hill. The egg was underneath the hill."

"Witchcraft" was written for an anthology that never saw print. So the story didn't, either—until now. But I liked the protagonist, jockey Deakin Kelley, so much that I decided to use him in a Jeri Howard novel called A Killing at the Track. *I'd wanted to write a horse racing mystery— probably due to the influence of all those Dick Francis novels I've read through the years, and those Kentucky Derby broadcasts on the first Saturday in May. As you read the story, hear the music in your head. "Witchcraft" is a song by Cy Coleman and Carolyn Leigh, sung most notably by Frank Sinatra, and it's about love. But love can be obsessive and dangerous, especially if you back the wrong horse.*

"Witchcraft" was written for an anthology that never saw print. So the story didn't, either—until now. But I liked the protagonist, jockey Deakin Kelley, so much that I decided to use him in a Jeri Howard novel called A Killing at the Track. *I'd wanted to write a horse racing mystery— probably due to the influence of all those Dick Francis novels I've read through the years, and those Kentucky Derby broadcasts on the first Saturday in May. As you read the story, hear the music in your head. "Witchcraft" is a song by Cy Coleman and Carolyn Leigh, sung most notably by Frank Sinatra, and it's about love. But love can be obsessive and dangerous, especially if you back the wrong horse.*

Witchcraft

When Deakin Kelley stepped onto the terrace, Sinatra's voice followed, singing "Witchcraft."

The words felt like fingers stroking the back of Deakin's neck. He walked to the railing and stood alone, glass in hand, sipping Scotch and looking out at the lights sprinkled over Beverly Hills. A full moon hung low in the sky.

He sang the words to the song, thinking he was alone. But he wasn't.

The woman's voice was a low flavorful whisper, somewhere to his right. "Let's dance," she said.

He glanced in her direction and liked what he saw. Hair dark as midnight fell to her sleek white shoulders. Along with a come-hither smile, she wore a green silk dress, slit high enough on the sides to give him an impressive view of her long legs. Her eyes were the same pale green as the jade pendant nestled between her breasts. Now she kicked off her shoes, held out her arms, and moved toward him, her feet bare on the terrazzo tile.

He left his glass on the railing, took her hand and circled her waist with his other. He guided her away from the circle of light cast by the lamp above the door, into the welcoming darkness at the end of the terrace. His body molded to hers as they swayed in time to the music. By the time Sinatra finished singing, he was bewitched.

"What's your name?" he asked, his mouth teasing the soft skin of her shoulder. He felt her fingers moving in his hair.

"Ann Barnstable," she whispered.

He backed away and looked up at her, dismayed. "You can't be Junior Barnstable's wife."

"You're right, I can't." She shook her head, then tilted it to one side. "I don't want to be. Who do you want me to be?"

"Just Ann."

"Plain Ann, then."

As she smiled, he thought there was nothing plain about her. The sight of her sent shivers down his spine. He could willingly drown in those green eyes. "I'm Deakin Kelley."

"I know who you are. Your reputation precedes you."

"Which reputation is that?" He was only half-joking. He already knew the answer.

"For being sharp-tongued, difficult to work with. For cutting a very wide swath through the female population." She looked amused. "But you're the hottest jockey on the track. At least this year. That's why my husband hired you to ride his horses."

"Sam Rogers hired me." Deakin retrieved his Scotch from the railing and took a swallow. "He's the trainer, the one who called my agent. I've known Sam a long time. But I don't know your husband. Except he's rich, and lives in San Marino." Now it was his turn to smile. "I have to wonder about a grown man who lets people call him Junior."

"His name's Arthur. But everyone calls him Junior, except the board of directors at that company he inherited from Senior."

"I'll bet they call him Junior behind his back," Deakin said. "What do you call him?"

"I don't call him anything at all. I talk to him as little as possible."

She looked over his shoulder, at the partygoers inside the house. Their host was a Hollywood producer who owned a couple of thoroughbreds Deakin rode regularly. That's why he'd been invited to the party. He wondered why she was here. Then she moved toward him again and he stopped wondering.

He reached up and cupped her face in his hand. Then he kissed her and he felt as though he'd been stripped bare.

"I want you."

Her mouth caressed his ear. "Let's go someplace where we can be alone."

He was more than ready. "Where?"

"I'm staying at my sister's place in Pasadena. She's out of town, but I've got a key. She lets me come and go when the family manse gets to be too much." She held his hand tightly, then released it as though she were reluctant to do so. "Lately it's too much."

Deakin gazed into her eyes. "I'll meet you downstairs in ten minutes."

She nodded, reaching for her discarded shoes. She slipped them on, then disappeared into the darkness.

Deakin returned to the house. The party was in full cry, shrill voices drowning out the music. Just as well. Whoever was closest to the CD player had abandoned Sinatra for some jarring noise full of pounding drums and over-amped guitars.

The room was gray with cigarette smoke, and he coughed. That's why he'd gone out on the terrace. Ever since he'd quit smoking, the second-hand smoke bothered him, and being around cigarettes gave him nicotine cravings that were hard to fight, as hard as the craving for Ann that now had him in its possession. He unloaded the Scotch glass on a passing waiter and looked around for his host, so he could say goodnight and make his escape.

Over the layers of noise, he heard a voice he recognized. Ruy Camacho was his chief rival in the jockey's room and on the tracks at Santa Anita, Hollywood Park and Del Mar. And for the attentions of several women, if the truth be told. Ruy had a thin dark face and the cold gaze of a predator. Right now he had a woman on each arm, holding them possessively as if he didn't want to share. Ruy's dark eyes glanced at Deakin. One black eyebrow quirked, and his mouth curved into a mocking smile, as though he knew what had gone on out on the terrace.

Deakin turned away, then caught sight of his host. He stepped past a couple of turf writers, dodged a trainer who was trying to chat up a blonde who had a secondary role in a new TV sitcom, and brushed past an actor who'd been famous twenty years ago. When he reached the producer, he said goodnight and hurried down to the crowded driveway, where Ann was waiting for him.

When Deakin got home it was past one in the morning. Ann's scent clung to him like the glow he'd felt after they'd made love. He hadn't wanted to leave her there in the big bed at her sister's house, where they'd talked for hours, about everything. He'd hated to leave. But he had to be at the track early. He had things to do.

He lived in a comfortable three-bedroom house on a quiet street in Arcadia. But when he parked his car in the driveway and got out, it didn't seem quiet. The lights were ablaze, and he could hear the TV all the way out here. He quickly unlocked the door that opened onto the den. His father sat on the sofa, staring at the screen, probably without seeing anything. Deakin quickly grabbed the remote and turned off the set. That's all he needed, another noise complaint from the neighbors.

"Dad." His voice sounded harsh in the sudden silence. "It's late. Why aren't you in bed?"

The old man looked at him without recognition. What

remained of his untidy white hair stuck up in clumps. His skinny frame was enveloped by a pair of baggy blue pajamas and a faded plaid robe. His feet were jammed into a pair of scuffed slippers.

"Mae's not here." Bert Kelley's voice creaked like a rusty hinge. "She's gone to the market."

Not again, Deakin thought sourly, at the mention of his mother's name. Mae Kelley had gone to the market for the last time more than eight years ago. She'd never made it home. A truck speeding through a red light had broadsided her car. She'd died en route to the emergency room. But the old man forgot, about that and a lot of other things. He forgot more and more lately.

Deakin looked around him, noting the shabby condition of the den and the adjoining kitchen. Dishes were piled in the sink and on every available surface. The old man's behavior had become increasingly erratic over the past month or so, to the point where Deakin knew he should hire someone to look after him. The elder Kelley hadn't been this difficult when Deakin's sister Ginny was looking after him. But Ginny was a staff sergeant in the Army. A year ago she'd gotten orders to Germany, and caregiver duties had passed to her brother.

So much for Deakin's single, carefree life, the one he'd become accustomed to. Now the old man hung around his neck, like a stone that got heavier with each passing month. Deakin was gone a lot, riding horses all over the country. When he was here, he watched his father change. Though crotchety, the old man had once been able to care for himself. Now he forgot to get out of bed, and when he did, he didn't bother to get dressed. Frequently he forgot to eat. Or when he fixed something for himself, disaster hovered, like the time he'd let a saucepan of soup boil dry and damn near set fire to the kitchen cabinets.

Deakin gazed at his father, inwardly chafing at the layers of family obligation on his shoulders, put there by circumstance and need. I never liked you much, old man. You're a hard-shelled old bastard and you made my mother miserable. But I can't just stick you into a nursing home. Not yet. I promised Ginny.

He fought back his irritation and the fatigue that threatened to swamp him. Instead he got the old man to his feet, steering him toward the back bedroom. The mess could wait. He had a housecleaner come in once a week, and tomorrow was the day. After he'd put his father to bed, he stripped off his clothes and fell into his own bed, making sure both the alarm clocks on the bedside table were set.

But sleep eluded him. He tossed restlessly in the sheets, his mind crackling as he remembered Ann, the feel of her body entwined with his.

Her face segued into his father's seamed and staring visage. Deakin sat upright in bed, sweat dampening his naked flesh. Damn. He'd been troubled by insomnia off and on for years. Tonight he should be tired enough to sleep but he couldn't.

He swung his legs to the floor and stalked into his bathroom, opening the medicine cabinet. Where was that stuff the doctor had prescribed? He found the amber plastic pharmacy bottle and looked at it. The stuff had to be taken sparingly, since he didn't want the drug to be in his system when he was riding horses. But if he didn't get some sleep, he'd be useless. He twisted off the cap, swallowed one of the capsules and washed it down with water. Then he went back to bed and stared at the ceiling until the drug overtook him.

It seemed like such a short time later that the alarm clocks jangled him into consciousness. When he got to Santa Anita later that morning, Deakin found Sam Rogers at the rail,

watching one of Junior Barnstable's horses being exercised. The colt was a big well-proportioned bay who looked like he could tear up the track. As Deakin walked toward the trainer he felt a momentary surge of regret for what he was about to do.

"That's the horse I want you to ride in the Santa Anita Derby," Sam drawled as Deakin joined him at the rail.

"We need to talk about that," Deakin began. Then he stopped.

Two people were walking toward them. The man, he knew, was Arthur Barnstable, known to everyone as Junior, the man who owned Barnstable Industries as well as a stable of expensive thoroughbreds. He was tall and thin, in his early fifties, with a sharp-featured face and thinning blond hair. Today he was dressed in slacks and sports jacket, casual but expensively tailored. On his arm was a slender blonde in beige slacks and shirt. She also wore a lot of chunky gold jewelry.

"Here's Junior now." Sam jerked his chin toward the approaching couple.

"Who's the woman?" As the words were out of his mouth, Deakin recognized her, the wrench in his gut telling him what his eyes had already identified. Oh, no, not Lina Pasmore. He hadn't seen her since the end of their affair, when he was riding at Miami area tracks.

The blonde hair had thrown him. The last time he'd seen Lina, she was a brunette. Edging toward forty, she was twice-divorced, lived in Fort Lauderdale, and drove a Jaguar as fast as she lived. She had money to burn, an appetite for kinky sex, and a penchant for jockeys. An exhilarating ride, but it had palled quickly. He was more than ready to bail out of the relationship when his agent, Nate Abernathy, had called with several offers of steady rides in California. He'd barely gotten settled here when he'd taken on the added burden of his father.

Now Lina Pasmore and Junior Barnstable joined Rogers and Deakin at the rail. Junior gazed admiringly at his bay colt. Lina, with a wicked glint in her blue eyes and a sly smile tweaking her full red lips, gazed at Deakin as though she'd like to do more than look.

What the hell was she doing here? Was she involved with Barnstable now?

Deakin fought to keep his face blank while Sam Rogers introduced Junior Barnstable, who had a pair of genial blue eyes above his thin patrician nose. He shook the owner's hand, as briefly and perfunctorily as possible. Junior turned to the woman at his side.

"Sam, Deakin," Junior said, "I'd like you to meet my sister, Lina Pasmore."

Sister?

Somewhere in the replay of last night, Deakin heard Ann's voice, telling him about her life as they lay together in the aftermath of their lovemaking. She was telling him about the house in San Marino she shared with her husband, a big one, thank God, because her mother-in-law—that harpy—lived there as well. And, she'd added, her witchy sister-in-law had just arrived for an extended visit. Which was one reason Ann had gone to stay for a few days at her sister Sheila's house in Pasadena.

Lina was Junior's sister? Shit.

"Hello, Deakin." Her voice was silky, smooth, intimate. She leaned closer. "It's nice to see you again, lover. I've been hoping we could get reacquainted."

That will be a cold day in hell, he thought.

"You two know each other?" Junior Barnstable asked, looking bemused. Deakin wondered if he knew his sister

had a thing for jockeys.

Junior reached into his back pocket, took out a small silver flask and unscrewed it. Word around the track was that he always carried it, ready to take a nip of his favorite bourbon. He poured a shot and offered it to his sister. Lina shook her head.

A meaty hand dropped onto Deakin's shoulder, saving him from actually having to respond to Junior's question. He turned and saw his agent, looking rumpled as usual. Nate Abernathy had missed a spot shaving that morning, and he had a coffee stain on the front of his shirt.

Nate greeted the others, then turned to Deakin. "Got a message you wanted to talk to me."

"Yeah, I do." Deakin excused himself and walked along the railing, Nate beside him. He felt Lina's eyes boring a hole in his back. When they were far enough away, Deakin stopped and turned to Nate. "I can't ride Barnstable's horses."

Nate gaped at him. "You're not serious. This guy's got major bucks and a stable of terrific nags. Sam Rogers is one of the best trainers going. And you're the best jockey. You can't turn it down." He gestured toward the splendid bay colt on the track. "That nag out there's got a chance at the Triple Crown. Don't be going prima donna on me, Deak."

Deakin shook his head. "Believe me, Nate, it's not that. It's personal."

"Personal? What the hell is that supposed to mean?"

It means I can't ride the man's horses and sleep with his wife at the same time, Deakin thought. That much remained of his conscience.

"Personal means personal, Nate. I can't talk about it."

Nate was fuming. "Personal better be goddamn good. What am I gonna tell Barnstable? And Sam Rogers?"

"I don't care what you tell Junior," Deakin snapped. "I'll tell Sam myself."

He looked back in the direction he'd come. Junior Barnstable and Lina Pasmore had departed. Where, he didn't know. He didn't much care. Sam Rogers had resumed his watch at the rail, calling out to the young woman who was working the bay. Deakin left Nate and walked back to the trainer. He took a deep breath and said what he had to say.

"It's not your dad, is it?" Sam asked. Deakin shook his head, feeling guilty at Sam's misplaced concern. "Well, I hate to lose you, son. But you do what you have to. I'll deal with Junior."

By the end of the day, Nate informed him disconsolately that Junior Barnstable had hired Ruy Camacho to ride his thoroughbreds. When Deakin got home, he discovered that the housecleaner hadn't shown up. Instead she'd left a message on the machine, claiming she was sick. Worse, his father hadn't even gotten out of bed, not even to go to the bathroom.

Grim-faced and feeling as though his already stretched nerves were twanging like piano wire, Deakin got the old man into the shower, then dressed him in a clean pair of pajamas. He ripped the soiled sheets and mattress pad from the bed, dumping the whole mess into the washer. As soon as he'd made the bed with fresh linen, he hauled out the Yellow Pages and started looking at the listings for nurses and nurses' registries. Before he could make some calls, the phone rang. It was Ann.

"I have to see you," she said.

Her words triggered a heat so intense he thought it would engulf him. But he looked at the old man sitting in front of the TV. "I can't. Last night I told you about my father. He's really bad today. I can't leave him."

"I'll be there in an hour. I'll bring dinner." Her voice soothed him with its evident sympathy. At that moment he felt he'd do anything for her.

Which included cleaning house. By the time Ann showed up with a bag of groceries, he had the place looking halfway decent and had fed his father some soup. She looked as beautiful in her jeans and T-shirt as she had the night before in her green silk dress. Conscious of a jockey's ever-present need to keep his weight down, she made a salad for both of them. While they ate, he told her what had happened at the track.

"I feel badly that you gave up those rides on my account," Ann said.

"To hell with it. There are always other horses." He gathered up the plates and carried them to the kitchen.

Ann followed him and opened the dishwasher. "I moved into Sheila's house." She took a deep breath. "Permanently."

Deakin stopped rinsing dishes, surprised, and yet wanting this. "You didn't have to do that on my account. You're sure?"

"I've never been more sure of anything in my life." Her green eyes gazed at him. "What about you?"

Whatever remained of his defenses gave way. "I love you. I want to be with you. You could move in here, except . . ." He stopped and glanced into the family room, where his father sat staring at the TV. He didn't want to talk about that now, didn't want to say words like Alzheimer's or senile dementia. He wanted to talk about Ann and what was happening between them. "Your sister doesn't mind? I mean, you said she was only out of town for a couple of days."

"Sheila?" Ann shook her head. "I talked with her this afternoon. She says it's about time I left Arthur. She's right. I've just been going through the motions."

"How did Junior take it?"

She didn't answer right away. "I didn't tell him," she said

finally. At the look on Deakin's face, she rushed to explain. "It's not the right time. He's busy with his mother." She shuddered. "She's a grasping old witch. Never approved of me. Not in the least. And I told you about his sister, who gives me the creeps."

You're not the only one, Deakin thought. "You've got to tell him. You're going to get a lawyer, aren't you? And file for divorce?"

"It's not as though he cares." She stuck her hands into the pockets of her jeans and leaned against the counter. "We've only been married three years. He unloaded his first wife years ago. I'm the trophy wife, the younger, more attractive model, strictly for show."

"You said last night you'd worked for him, as a secretary."

She nodded. "Administrative assistant. At his corporate headquarters, in downtown LA. I was good at it. Should have stayed there. But . . . I thought I was in love. I've never been married before and I thought this was the man of my dreams. So urbane and elegant."

And so rich. The thought came unbidden and Deakin banished it quickly. She wasn't like that. Not his Ann.

"I never figured Junior to be all that elegant," he joked. "But what the hell do I know? I'm just a hick from Colorado."

Ann grinned. "He's got a certain distinguished captain of industry charm. When he wants to. He was displaying quite of bit of it when he courted me. And I fell for it. Everyone told me how lucky I was, making such a catch. Of course his mother had a fit. She and the lawyers made sure I signed a prenuptial agreement."

"So you don't get anything if you divorce him?"

"A small settlement. More than generous, certainly more than I was making as his assistant. But I don't care about the money." She shook her head. "I know a lot of people wouldn't believe that. They'd think I was just a gold-digger, a younger woman marrying an older man for his money. But it's not like that. I'm miserable. I knew it was a mistake but I . . . I'm afraid of him. I don't want to set him off."

"Afraid of him?" Deakin frowned. "Why?"

She ducked her head, then lifted it, and he saw fear in her pale green eyes. "Sometimes he hits me."

"The son of a bitch," Deakin said, angry enough to go after Junior right now.

Ann smiled again. "Believe me, if you'd ever met his mother, you'd know just how true that is."

"How can you joke about it?"

"It's the only way to survive. Please don't ever tell anyone. I don't want anyone to know that he treats me that way. You and Sheila are the only people I've told. She's been telling me ever since the first time that I should walk out on him. But I haven't had the strength to." She reached for him. "Until now."

Deakin and Ann managed to keep their relationship a secret all of three weeks. During that time Lina Pasmore was a frequent visitor to the track. Whenever she encountered Deakin she made it clear she was interested in resuming their affair. Deakin made it just as plain he wasn't. Finally he heard a rumor she was boffing Ruy Camacho. Served them both right, as far as he was concerned.

During the same three weeks Deakin hired and fired two home care workers. He finally settled on a licensed practical nurse named Wanda. She seemed steady and reliable, a capable middle-aged woman who instantly developed a rapport with his father.

With someone dealing with the old man, Deakin spent as much time as he could with Ann, both at his place and at

Sheila's house in Pasadena. Sheila traveled a lot, selling fitness equipment and going to karate tournaments. She resembled Ann, who was younger. Both women had dark brown hair, but Sheila's eyes were blue. Where Ann was slender, Sheila had muscles. The row of karate trophies on her shelves showed how she kept them toned.

Ann was still waiting for the right time to tell Junior she wanted a divorce. Before the right time came, they were strolling hand-in-hand on Venice Beach when they were spotted by Ruy Camacho, who evidently took great pleasure in spreading the news of the affair all over the track.

"Are you crazy?" Nate said with a scowl as soon as he heard about it.

"I don't think so." Deakin kept his voice low and level, determined not to be provoked.

"Common sense . . ." Nate began, but Deakin brushed his words aside.

"To hell with common sense. I told you it was personal, Nate. I don't want to discuss it."

Everyone else was discussing it, though. Deakin was getting plenty of wise-ass remarks from the guys in the jockey's room. That he could take. He was used to their banter, friendly or not. Then a couple of the turf writers, ones he'd had run-ins with in the past, made the connection with Deakin's earlier short-lived agreement to ride Junior Barnstable's horses and speculated in print and innuendo as to why the jockey had backed out of the deal.

Lina Pasmore intercepted him as he left the jockey room late Thursday afternoon. "I have to wonder about your judgment, lover," she said. "I know you like to take risks." She gave him that sly smile again. "But do you really want to get in my brother's sights?"

"I'm not afraid of your brother."

52

She laughed. "You always did have spirit, lover. That's why I liked you so much. Maybe Junior should be afraid of you."

He glared at her and headed for the parking lot. That evening, his father was querulous during dinner. He kept muttering to himself, and asking when the pretty lady was coming to visit again.

"You mean Ann?" Deakin asked. "Or Wanda?" Not that he'd consider the middle-aged nurse pretty. Solid and comfortable were more like it.

"Ann?" The old man repeated. "Pretty lady with blue eyes."

"Ann has green eyes."

"Blue eyes, green eyes," Bert Kelley said in a singsong voice. "Skinny lady, pretty lady."

"Ann's a curvy lady, Dad." Deakin shook his head. The old man was drifting out of reality again. After cleaning up the dishes, he put the old man to bed and headed for his own room. The phone rang late, rousing him from sleep. It was midnight, he realized, staring bleary-eyed at the clock.

"I think you'd better get over here." It was Sheila, Ann's sister.

"What happened?"

"It's Ann. Oh, hell, just get over here."

He dressed quickly, grabbed his keys, and pointed his car toward the freeway. When he got to Pasadena, Sheila greeted him at the door.

"I just got back from a business trip," she told Deakin. "I found her like this. She won't go to a doctor."

He pushed past her and headed for Ann's bedroom. The room was dark, but he could see the outline of her body as she lay huddled on top of the bed. He switched on the light. "Jesus Christ!"

53

"Turn it off," she cried, clutching the green silk robe around her.

He moved to the bed and gently caught her wrists. She winced, and so did he. He pulled open the robe, appalled at the black and purple bruises that marred the milky soft skin of her abdomen. He'd taken plenty of falls at the track, had been stepped on by a few horses, and hadn't given the injuries more than a passing thought. But to see Ann like this made the anger in him boil to the surface.

He looked at her face, unmarked except for tears and reddened eyes. "Did he do this to you? Was it Junior?"

"Of course it was Junior," Sheila said behind him, her voice edged with disgust. "He's all pissed off because he heard about the two of you."

"I'll kill the son of a bitch." It was all he could do to spit out the words.

"Be my guest," Sheila said, her face grim. "I'd like to punch him out myself. The creep's got it coming. You notice the asshole was careful not to hit her face. He always is."

"How the hell did he get in?" Deakin demanded.

A look passed from Ann to Sheila, then Sheila answered. "Ann says it was about seven when someone knocked. She checked the peephole, didn't see anyone, then opened the door to investigate. That's when he forced his way in. I told her she should call the cops or go to a hospital, but she won't listen. See if you can talk some sense into her."

He tried to persuade her to either course of action, but she refused. He wound up spending what was left of the night lying next to her on the bed, careful not to jostle her, unable to sleep because of the rage that kept him awake.

Deakin thought he'd be able to keep his cool at the track. But then he saw Junior Barnstable in the Paddock Gardens

Friday morning, talking with Sam Rogers and Ruy Camacho. The older man looked cool, unconcerned and completely in control, not at all like a man who'd battered his wife the evening before.

Deakin didn't remember the rest of it clearly. All he knew was that he'd backed Barnstable into the fence. He recalled the sound of his own voice threatening to kill Junior if he ever laid a hand on Ann again. He saw the horrified looks on the faces of Sam Rogers and several other bystanders, felt the hands of Ruy Camacho and another jockey pulling him away from Barnstable, toward the jockey room.

"Are you out of your fucking mind?" Ruy hissed into his ear once they were inside. "The stewards will set you down for sure."

"He beat her up," Deakin said. "He broke into the house where she was staying and beat her up."

"You're kidding." Ruy's disbelief was evident.

"You think I'd lie about something like that? I saw her. I know what kind of bruises a fist makes."

Ruy shrugged matter-of-factly. "He's such a cold fish I didn't think he had the *cojones*." Then a frown passed over his narrow dark face. "Didn't think he cared whether his wife was screwing you or not. Didn't think she cared if anyone knew. I mean . . ."

Deakin wheeled on him. "What the hell do you mean?"

"Don't mean nothin', man." Ruy held up his hands and backed away. "You want to self-destruct in front of witnesses, ain't no skin off my ass."

"Hey, Kelley." Deakin turned and saw one of the other jocks in the doorway. "Stewards want to see you. Right now."

The stewards told him he was getting off easy with a suspension, since Mr. Barnstable had graciously declined to press charges for assault and battery. Deakin went back to the jockey room, ignoring the stares and the whispers he encountered en route. He collected his gear, went home and called Ann.

"What are you doing at home?" she asked, sounding better than she had last night. "I hope you didn't do anything crazy at the track today." He gave her an edited version, but even that was bad enough. "Oh, Deak, no. You played right into his hands."

"I know, I know. It was stupid. But I saw him and I just lost it."

"My poor darling, what I have I gotten you into?"

"The hell with it. I don't care. How are you feeling? I'll come over . . ."

She sighed. "After your outburst at the track? That's not a good idea. It's probably better if we don't see each other for awhile, until all the talk dies down."

"Okay," he said reluctantly, not liking it at all. But he could see the sense in it.

He hung up the phone in his bedroom and went out to the den where his father sat in front of the TV while Wanda knitted. Suddenly he wanted to be alone, or as alone as he could be in this house. "Take the rest of the day, Wanda," he told the LPN. "I'll see you tomorrow."

It wasn't Wanda he saw when he answered the door the next morning, however. Two plainclothes police officers showed him their badges. In detached voices they informed him Junior Barnstable had been found dead late Friday night, slumped in the driver's seat of his Mercedes, parked in the lot at the racetrack.

"How did he die?" Deakin reeled back into his living room. He had a queasy feeling in the pit of his stomach.

"We'll know more after the autopsy," the older cop said,

not really answering his question. "Mr. Kelley, I understand you and Mr. Barnstable had an altercation yesterday at the track. What was that about?"

Deakin stumbled over the words, the picture of his hot-headed attack on Junior looking worse as he told it. When the detectives asked him where he'd been the previous night, he got worried. Home alone with a senile old man didn't seem like much of an alibi. Did he need an alibi?

Finally the cops left, and he got on the phone to Nate Abernathy. The agent sounded worried. "It looks real bad, what with you jumping on Junior like that. There were a lot of witnesses. Sam Rogers, Ruy Camacho, a couple other owners and trainers. It's bad enough you got involved with the man's wife, but then you threaten to kill him. What the hell got into you?"

"He beat up Ann. He broke into the house where she was staying and knocked her around."

"Junior?" Nate sounded uncertain. "I can't believe he'd do something like that. He seemed like such a nice guy. You're sure she's being straight with you?"

"You think Junior Barnstable would broadcast the fact that he used his wife for a punching bag? Ann couldn't have lied. I know what I saw."

"I just hope this was a heart attack, a stroke, something like that. There's a lot of rumors and nasty talk going around the track. And it's all about you."

Deakin stopped answering the phone by mid-afternoon. He told Wanda just to let the answering machine pick up the calls. He kept hoping Ann would call but she didn't. By dinnertime the guys with the TV cameras showed up on his lawn and what little of the news he watched had a lot of speculation about the sudden death of Arthur Barnstable. He went to bed early but couldn't sleep. In his bathroom he yanked open the medicine cabinet, looking for his sleeping pills.

The amber plastic container was nearly empty. That was odd. He'd just gotten the prescription refilled, three, four weeks ago, right before he met Ann.

The autopsy showed that Junior had died of an overdose of sleeping pills. The same kind Deakin took. The cops came back, with a search warrant. They took the prescription bottle, with his name on the label, sealed in a plastic evidence bag. They also extended an invitation, the sort one didn't refuse, to come down to the police station for further questioning.

He didn't have an attorney, so Nate found one. He was a sandy-haired guy in a brown suit who had a habit of drumming his fingers on his desk as he talked.

"The cops did talk with Mrs. Barnstable," he told Deakin. "You say she told you her husband broke into her sister's house around seven o'clock Thursday night and beat her. But there are five witnesses at Barnstable Industries in Century City who say Mr. Barnstable was in a meeting with them all evening. The meeting began at five and didn't break until eight-thirty. At no time did Mr. Barnstable leave."

"Maybe Ann was mistaken about the time," Deakin said in a hollow voice. "Maybe he went there after his meeting."

The lawyer shook his head. "Mr. Barnstable met his sister and a friend for dinner at a restaurant in Beverly Hills. The waiter confirms it. Then they went back to San Marino. It looks like he never went near the Pasadena house."

Deakin couldn't believe what he was hearing. "But the bruises. I saw them. So did Sheila."

The lawyer looked troubled now. "Mrs. Barnstable's sister —Sheila—is out of town. The police spoke with Mrs. Barnstable. She made no complaint to them about her husband beating her. When they asked her about injuries, she said she slipped in her sister's kitchen and stumbled over a chair." At the look on his client's face, he shrugged. "I'm just telling you what the cops told me. I haven't actually talked with Mrs. Barnstable myself. She's moved back into the San Marino house and she's making arrangements for her husband's funeral. I left a message for her. I'd also like to talk with Mrs. Pasmore, the sister-in-law. But I understand she's staying with a friend in Monrovia."

Mrs. Pasmore. Lina. Of course. She was Junior's alibi for the night Ann had been beaten. She knew about his insomnia, the sleeping pills. And she must have come to his house. His father had told him, but he hadn't listened because he thought the old man was wandering. A pretty lady with blue eyes had been to the house. That had to be Lina.

He had a good idea who Lina's friend in Monrovia was. That's where Ruy Camacho lived. That night he waited, his car parked across the street from Ruy's townhouse. It was late when he saw the Porsche pull into the driveway. Ruy and Lina got out. He wore jeans and a pullover, Lina wore slacks and a shirt. Their laughter carried in the still night air as they walked toward the front door, arms around each other. She didn't look like a woman who grieved much for her brother.

Deakin caught up with them as they reached the door. Ruy turned, keys in hand, his eyes wary and ready for trouble. He looked Deakin up and down, but he didn't say anything.

"Well, isn't this just a cozy little threesome," Lina purred, hands on her hips. "You look all in, lover. You want a drink?"

"I want to talk."

Ruy pushed open the door and beckoned him to enter. The living room was decorated in stark modern, with lots of angular teak furniture. Ruy flicked on the track lighting and stepped to the bar, pouring a glass of wine for Lina. He handed her the glass, then poured a couple of shots of Scotch, one for himself and one for Deakin. He held one glass at arm's length. Deakin stared at the glass as though the contents had been poisoned. Then he reached for it and downed the liquor.

Lina kicked off her shoes and sat cross-legged on Ruy's sofa, one hand toying with the undone buttons at the top of her linen shirt. "It's your dime, lover," she told Deakin.

"I didn't kill your brother," he said.

Lina took a sip from her wine glass, then set it down on the end table. "I didn't think so, lover. It's not your style. Besides, while you may have had a motive, I can't figure when you'd have had the opportunity. That's why the police haven't actually arrested you. The drug was in his flask of bourbon. How would you have put it there? After that little scene Friday morning, it's not likely my brother would allow you into his car. Nor would he let you slip him a cocktail full of pharmaceuticals."

Ruy drank his Scotch and set the glass on the bar. Then he stood behind the sofa, his hand gently massaging her shoulders. "Word around the track is you faked it."

"Faked what?"

"Threatening Junior," Ruy said impatiently. "So you'd get suspended. That way you're off the track when he gets the overdose. Makes it look like you didn't have the opportunity."

"Bullshit," Deakin said. "I wasn't faking that."

"I know you weren't. I'm the guy pulled you off him, remember?"

"We have to look at who did have the opportunity to lay hands on that flask." Lina narrowed her blue eyes as she looked at Deakin.

"You did." He flung the words at her like a challenge.

"I suppose so," she conceded. "But there's someone else.

60

Someone with a motive. And we both know who that is. My dear sister-in-law Ann."

"I don't believe it." Deakin glared at her.

Lina smiled. "She signed a prenuptial agreement, lover. If she'd divorced Junior, she'd have gotten nothing but a small settlement. But now that he's dead, she'll get a very large bundle. Last time I saw her, which was this morning, she was planning to run the whole damn company. I must say, she could have waited till after the funeral."

"What about you? Don't you benefit from his death?"

"Not really. My father took care of both of us in his will." She shrugged. "Oh, I know Junior left me something. But the bulk of his estate goes to Ann."

He didn't want to believe it. He lashed out. "I wouldn't trust you as far as I could throw you."

"Why would you want to throw me, lover? Seems like a waste of energy." Lina leaned back and smiled up at Ruy. Then she looked at Deakin and her face turned serious. "You'd better trust me. I'm telling the truth. You've been set up."

"He beat her."

"He never touched her," Lina countered. "He was at the office. Then he had dinner with me and Ruy." The other jockey confirmed this with a curt nod. "No one beat Ann. She engineered it herself, so she could be sufficiently bruised to convince you."

"You could have taken the pills," Deakin said. "My father told me a pretty lady with blue eyes had been to the house."

"You're sure he didn't mean a pretty lady with green eyes?" Lina's mouth quirked. "One who'd been to your house many times, or so I hear. I've never been to your house. At least not the one here. What about Sheila, Ann's sister? She's got blue eyes. She's also something of a martial arts maven, or so I hear. She could probably land a few punches where they'd leave marks."

"How the hell would Ann know about the pills?" Deakin stopped. Had he told her about his insomnia?

"Of course she knew," Lina said. "She knew everything about you. Because I told her, last year when you and I were involved. Last time I came out here for a visit, she and I got together and dished. Girl talk, y'know. She asked all sorts of questions about you, lover. I told her about your father, your insomnia and those damned pills in your medicine cabinet. I even told her about that little mole on the inside of your thigh." Lina shook her head. "I had no idea she was going to make a move on you. Although it seems she had something on her mind besides sex."

Ruy seemed unmoved by Lina's recollection of her affair with Deakin. While she talked, his hands stroked her shoulders and she sighed pleasurably. But Ruy's face darkened with a frown. He addressed his words to Deakin. "You know that day I saw you and her at the beach? I got a phone call a couple of days before. Man, woman, I'm not sure. Said you were screwing an owner's wife and if I kept my eyes open, I'd see you with her. At Venice Beach."

"And since you're so fond of me," Deakin added, "you made sure everyone knew about it."

A grim smile flicked across Ruy's mouth. "Damn straight. But somebody else made sure everyone knew about the two of you. I did a little checking around. Seems I'm not the only guy who got one of those anonymous phone calls."

"Don't you see?" Lina asked. "She planned the whole thing. Getting into your bed. And murdering my brother."

He didn't want to see. But he was remembering the day he and Ann had gone to Venice. It was Ann's suggestion, a spurof-the-moment day trip. But had it been spontaneous? Now he was wondering.

Lina reached for her wine glass. "I don't know what else I can say to convince you. Except this. It's the money, lover. I don't need it. Ann does."

He turned and left Ruy's condo, and drove back towards home. Somehow he missed the exit and found himself driving along the streets of San Marino, to the big house where Ann had lived with Junior. The place was dark, but somewhere in the distance he heard music. He followed the sound, back through a gate that led to a garden. He made his way along a terrace overlooking a swimming pool, and saw a light and an open French door. It led to a study with book-lined walls. The music came from a radio on one of the shelves. Ann was seated at a desk in the middle of the room, her green silk robe pulled around her as she peered at the screen of a computer.

"All alone?" he asked.

She looked startled, then she got to her feet, crossed the room and stood before him. "Deakin. Darling, you shouldn't be here. What if the police find out?"

"You told them you fell in Sheila's kitchen. But that's not true."

She ducked her head the way she had before, and dark hair curtained her eyes. "Of course it isn't true. It's just that I didn't want anyone to know he'd hit me. I thought if people knew, they'd think . . ."

"That I killed him. That's what you had in mind all along."

He remembered the night they met, when she'd said, I know who you are. After talking with Lina, Ann's words now had darker implications. He reached out and untied the robe. She wore nothing underneath. He stared at the body that had mesmerized him. The bruises that had been so vivid a few days ago were fading. "Sheila hit you, to make it look good. She's in on it. What did you promise her, a generous slice of Barnstable Industries?"

"I can promise you more," she whispered.

The music changed. He heard a new song playing on the radio. He laughed when he recognized the lyrics. Sinatra. "Witchcraft." The words felt like claws raking down Deakin's back.

He reached up and cupped her face in his hand. Then he kissed her and he felt as though he'd been stripped bare.

"I want you." Her mouth caressed his ear. "Let's go someplace where we can be alone."

"No deal." He cast off her spell and moved toward the phone.

"Little Red Corvette" appeared in the anthology Lethal Ladies. *The story features my series protagonist, Oakland P.I. Jeri Howard, working on a case at the behest of Acey Collins, the biker-mechanic who appears in Jeri's third case,* Take A Number. *How did this one begin? Eavesdropping can be very instructive. I was having lunch at a deli in downtown Oakland, listening shamelessly as the two men at the next table talked about a car one of them wanted to buy. It was a classic car with low mileage that had been left at a repair shop and never claimed. I wondered why. I finished lunch and left before the men finished their conversation, so I was compelled to supply my own answers.*

Little Red Corvette

"Isn't she a beauty?" Acey Collins asked, admiration in his eyes and voice. "A '61. Cherry."

I looked at him, exasperated. We were standing on the corner of Thirty-Sixth and Broadway, in the heart of Oakland's Auto Row, just after noon on a blustery March day. Acey gazed at the repair shop on the corner with a look he usually reserved for his wife, his kids, or his Harley-Davidson. I followed the direction of his eyes and finally figured out that "she" was a car, a cherry red Chevrolet Corvette convertible, the car I associated with Tod and Buz and all those black-and-white reruns of *Route 66.*

"I wonder what the insurance would run on a car like that?"

My companion glared at me as though I'd committed heresy. He shook his head in disgust and folded his tattooed arms over his stringy chest. "You got no soul."

"What I do have is a limited amount of time, Acey. It's chilly, the wind is blowing. You brought me here to look at a car?"

"You got anything better to do?"

"It's lunch time, Acey. Eating comes to mind."

"So I'll buy you a hot dog."

"Yech. What's the gig, Acey?" I looked at my watch. "I have an appointment in thirty minutes. I'm a private investigator who drives a six-year-old Toyota. Why did you drag me away from my office to show a me a little red Corvette?"

"The Toyota could use a tune-up, you know." Acey tossed his head, setting his long gray-blond ponytail moving. He gave me a sly look, pale blue eyes glittering in his bearded face. "I heard it knocking when you pulled up. Those brakes were squealing some too."

"Is this leading somewhere?" I tapped both my foot and the face of my utilitarian Timex.

"I'm a good mechanic, Jeri. You do this for me, I'll work on your car."

That got my attention. The Toyota needed new shocks and I didn't like that sound the brakes made. I'd put off having any major work done because at the moment I had a cash flow problem. Acey's trade-off sounded good to me.

I pushed away seductive thoughts of new points and plugs. "What do I have to do?" I asked, suspicious.

"You're an investigator. I want you to investigate."

"A car? Back up and start at the beginning."

Acey took my arm and nudged me away from the corner like a border collie taking charge of a wayward sheep. "Come on, I don't want Musetta to see us." We moved back down Thirty-Sixth to where my Toyota was parked. I looked at its grimy paint and promised myself a trip to the car wash. *After* Acey worked on it.

"I'm in Musetta's shop a couple of days ago, looking to buy some parts," Acey said. "I see the Corvette. It's beautiful, a classic. Only eight hundred miles on it."

"A car that old?"

"Yeah. That's one anomaly."

Hearing the word "anomaly" come out of the mouth of this aging biker took me by surprise. "There are others?"

"Plenty. I know Del Musetta, from way back. His brother was at Folsom the same time I was doin' that stretch for receiving stolen property. The criminal gene runs deep in this family. I know what I'm talking about here."

"So how did Musetta get the Corvette in the first place? You think he stole it?"

"Maybe." Acey jerked his bearded chin back toward the repair shop. "He tells me the Corvette was left at the shop to be repaired, five years ago. Says nobody ever came to claim it. Says he got tired of it sitting around his shop so he decided to sell it."

"How much is he asking?"

Acey named a figure, several times what I'd paid for my Toyota, that made me wince. "That's a bundle."

"No, it ain't." Acey spoke with authority. "Not for that car. I could turn around and sell that Corvette for twice what he's asking. *If* Musetta is telling the truth, it's a good buy. But before I lay out that kind of money for that car, I want to know the deal is on the up-and-up."

He patted my trusty Toyota on the fender, tilted his head and squinted at me and smiled like a fisherman who'd just hooked a big one.

"You do this for me, Jeri, I'll fix this car so it purrs like a cat."

"You've got yourself a deal."

I returned to the repair shop that afternoon, after a spin through the California Civil Code. If the Corvette had been left at Musetta's for repairs and never claimed, the shop owner had what was called a possessory lien on the car. He was entitled to compensation for making repairs, performing labor, furnishing supplies and storing the vehicle. The lien dated from the time a written statement of charges for the completed work was presented to the Corvette's registered owner.

First question. Did Musetta ever try to find the owner?

The owner could extinguish the lien on the car by presenting the repairman with a cashier's check for the amount owed. If that didn't happen, Musetta could go to court or apply for authorization to conduct a lien sale within thirty days after the lien had arisen.

Second question. Had Musetta obtained authorization within the legal time limit?

For that he had to go to the Department of Motor Vehicles. It should be easy enough to check whether he'd made the request and paid the filing fee.

Acey said the garage owner told him the Corvette had been sitting at the garage for five years. That brought me to the third question. If Musetta had the legal right to sell the car, why had he waited so long?

The Corvette stood to one side of Musetta's shop, under an overhang. Seen this close, I had to agree with Acey. It was a beauty. Paint like a fat ripe cherry, glossy and shiny, complemented by gleaming chrome. Not a mark on it. I circled the car slowly, then I heard someone behind me. I turned and saw a bulky dark-haired man. He was about six feet tall and he carried a lot of excess weight around his middle. He wore a set of grimy blue coveralls with the name "Del" stitched in red above the left breast pocket.

"I couldn't resist a closer look," I said. "What a gorgeous car. Is it for sale?"

"Yeah, it is." He grinned. "You interested?"

"Well, that would depend on the price."

He named a figure, considerably higher than the one Acey had mentioned. First anomaly, I thought. Of course, Acey knows more about cars and what they're worth than I do, and the garage owner knew it. I looked like a better mark, someone who'd pay more for this flashy car.

"You don't normally sell cars, do you?" I looked around, then focused on Del, giving him a flirtatious smile. "How did you happen on this one?"

Del laughed, a big belly-rumbling sound. "There's a story about that. The guy just left the car here, coupla years back, for a tune-up and a brake job. I told him he could pick it up the next day. He never picked it up."

"How long ago was this?" I asked, frowning. "I mean, doesn't this person still own the car? How can you sell it?"

He rubbed a stubby-fingered hand across his bristly chin. "Oh, yeah, I got a lien. Unless the owner shows up and pays me what he owes me, the car belongs to me. Damn thing's been sitting here for three years."

Anomaly number two, I thought. He had told Acey he'd had the car five years.

"I thought about keeping it myself, but . . ." Del stopped and slapped his considerable girth. "It ain't my kinda car. I can't get this belly behind the wheel of a little sports job two-seater. Besides, I looked it up in the Blue Book. It's worth quite a bit. I'd just as soon sell it and get the money."

"It's my kind of car," I said, running a finger over the bright red finish, dangling the possibility that I might be willing to whip out my checkbook this very minute. "Didn't you ever try to find the owner?"

Now Musetta backpedaled. "Well, I called the phone number he left. Buncha times. Even went by his place but there wasn't anyone there."

I had a feeling the garage owner's efforts to find the Corvette's owner had been somewhat desultory and limited to right after the car was left at the garage. I let a bit of this show on my face. "Do you still have the work request?"

Musetta looked surprised. "Well, yeah. It's in the filing cabinet somewheres. Why?"

"Let me take a look at it."

"What you want to do that for?"

"I'm really interested in buying the car," I said, stroking my handbag as though it contained a large wad of cash. "But I'd feel much better if I tried to contact the owner myself."

Musetta frowned. "I told you, I called his place. Even went by there."

"Just for my own peace of mind." I flashed him a bright smile. "I really couldn't buy the car unless I was sure everything was legal."

"I'm telling ya, I got a lien on this car," Musetta protested. I sighed, shook my head and turned to go back to my Toyota. "Wait a minute. I guess there's no harm in letting you see it. Just proves my point."

I followed him into the grimy office of the repair shop, where the decor ran to calendars featuring flashy cars and naked female body parts. He opened the second drawer of a brown metal filing cabinet and rummaged through the contents. Finally he pulled out the work request and held it out for me to examine. He looked dismayed when I gently plucked it from his hand.

I quickly glanced at the total for the work performed. It was a hefty repair bill, but a fraction of what Musetta hoped to get by selling the Corvette. The date was smudged but it looked like April, three years ago. The person who left the Corvette to be repaired was one Raleigh Lambert. He lived at an address on Sea View Avenue in Piedmont, a small city completely surrounded by Oakland, where big well-tended houses hold court on the hills that rise above the city flatlands.

I wrote down the address and phone number. Then I handed the work request back to Musetta, gave him a big smile and told him I'd be back.

Whoever had named the street Sea View wasn't kidding. Big bucks, I thought, to go with the spectacular panorama of

San Francisco Bay visible from the front porch of Raleigh Lambert's gray stone house. I rang the bell. No answer. What had once been a well-tended English garden needed some work, I thought as I walked back down the steps to the curved driveway that led to a detached double garage. No cars, no movement behind the curtains on any of the big glass windows. It didn't look like anyone was home. The place had an aura of neglect.

I repaired to the Alameda County Courthouse for a stroll through the assessor's records. For the past two years, the property taxes on the Piedmont address had been paid by one Harold Baldwin. Three years ago they'd been paid by Raleigh Lambert. Had Lambert sold the house to Baldwin? When I went to the recorder's office to take a look at the real estate transactions, I didn't find one for the Sea View address.

I looked up from the microfilm reader and thought for a moment. Maybe Baldwin inherited the house from Lambert. I switched my search to the probate records. That's where I hit pay dirt. Raleigh Lambert was dead, and among the beneficiaries listed on his will was a nephew, Harold Baldwin.

Now I had the date of Lambert's death to compare with the smudged date on Musetta's work request. Lambert left the Corvette for repairs a week before he died. When I called the Department of Motor Vehicles, there was no record of any authorization issued to the garage owner to conduct a lien sale. Musetta had no right to sell the car. In fact, he could be charged with conversion. Harold Baldwin was the legal owner of that little red Corvette.

It was past five when I parked on the street outside the house on Sea View, with a clear view of the porch and garage. Fifteen minutes later a silver Jaguar approached and turned into the curved driveway. By the time the driver was out of the car and walking toward the house, I was there to intercept him.

"Harold Baldwin?"

He was medium all over, height, weight, and age, with short brown hair and brown eyes, wearing gray slacks and a blue sweater, both of which looked expensive but didn't fit him very well. He smiled politely and looked a bit wary at being accosted by a strange woman in his own driveway. "Yes?"

"It's about your uncle and a car," I began. Then I stopped. There had to be some reason for the look that flickered in the man's eyes. Maybe it was my imagination, or a trick of the light on this March evening. But I was sure his expression had migrated from polite disinterest to something else. Could it be panic?

Right now Baldwin had masked whatever it was and gone back to the polite smile. "My uncle and a car?" he repeated.

I did a quick edit on my words. "Your uncle is Raleigh Lambert?"

"Was. Uncle Raleigh died three years ago."

"Well, that explains it," I said cheerfully. "He left a car at a repair shop on Broadway. A red Corvette. And he never picked it up." Harold Baldwin looked blank. "You didn't know?"

"My uncle was something of a collector." Baldwin frowned. It made him look sulky. "He had so many cars. I do seem to recall a Corvette. I assumed he'd sold it. Who are you?"

"Jeri Howard." I decided not to mention I was a private investigator. "I saw the car at the repair shop and the owner told me it was for sale. He claims he owns it because it was left there and no one picked it up. The work request gave me Mr. Lambert's name and address. So I guess you really own the car, as long as you pay the repair bill."

I smiled again and hoped Harold Baldwin wouldn't ask how I'd figured out he was Raleigh Lambert's nephew and heir to the red Corvette. As it was he seemed preoccupied by what I'd just told him.

"How did your uncle die?" I asked. "It must have been quite unexpected."

"An accident."

I made a sympathetic noise and looked at Baldwin expectantly, waiting for details. With any luck I'd unnerved him to the point that he would say almost anything, just in the hope that I'd go away.

"Yes, right here at the house." He peered at his gold Rolex. "I really must go, Ms. . . . ?"

"Howard."

"Yes, uh, where is this repair shop? I'll have my attorney look into the matter."

I gave him Musetta's name and address, regretting a bit that the cat was out of that particular bag. But since I'd already mentioned it at the outset, there didn't seem to be any way to avoid it.

The next morning I left my Adams Point apartment and headed for the Oakland Public Library where copies of the Oakland *Tribune* were available on microfilm. I backtracked to April, three years ago, hoping that whatever tragic accident had taken Raleigh Lambert's life had rated a mention. If it hadn't I would be reduced to poring through the obituary notices.

I was saved from that fate by a front-page headline informing me that the previous owner of the red Corvette had met the Grim Reaper at the wheel of another of his classic cars, this one a '65 Mustang. But he hadn't been on the streets of Piedmont. Instead, the 72-year-old Lambert, had driven the car into the garage, lowered the door and died of carbon monoxide poisoning.

Lambert was described by the *Tribune* as a retired Oakland businessman. From what I read, he was considered quite the man-about-town. He collected fine porcelain and classic cars. On a Thursday evening in early April, he'd attended a dance at the Claremont Hotel with Mrs. Patricia Wong, described as an old family friend. The body had been found Friday morning by another friend, Teo Martinez. Nephew Harold told the police that his uncle had recently been diagnosed with liver cancer. Lambert's physician confirmed this.

Accident or suicide? I wondered. I moved the microfilm forward but didn't find any other articles about Lambert's death, just the obituary notice which gave the time and date of his funeral.

Small as it is, Piedmont does have its own police force. Sergeant Fleming, the officer who'd investigated Lambert's death, looked like a yuppie lawyer rather than a detective. He was quite bemused when I told him I was a private investigator.

"Most of my time I deal with burglaries and nuisance complaints," he said. "Don't see many dead bodies up here."

"I read the initial report of the incident in the *Tribune*. There seemed to be some question whether it was accidental or suicide."

"We finally ruled that an accidental death. There was alcohol in his system, he was elderly, coming home from a dance, so he may have been tired and less alert that he normally would have been. Lambert had one of those gizmos that opened and closed his garage door. It looked like he'd hit it before he got out of the car and had been overcome by the carbon monoxide. I think he probably hit that garage door button by mistake and didn't even realize what was happening."

"But the nephew, Harold Baldwin, thought it might be suicide."

Fleming nodded. "Lambert's doctor said the cancer would have killed him in a year or eighteen months. So he could have committed suicide, even if his lady friend insisted that was impossible."

"Is that Mrs. Wong, the woman he was with the night he died?"

"Yeah. Lived around the corner from him, on Farragut Avenue. She said he wouldn't have killed himself. I didn't have a note to indicate a suicidal state of mind. Why are you asking about the Lambert case?"

"Any chance it might be murder?"

"Murder?" Fleming's eyebrows shot up. "We haven't had a murder in, oh twenty, twenty-five years. Way before my time, anyway."

The rich are different, I told myself, and Piedmont really was a world apart from Oakland. Fleming dropped the laid-back yuppie persona. "What makes you think anyone killed Raleigh Lambert?"

"My suspicious nature, I guess. Tell me, where was Harold Baldwin the night his uncle died?"

"At home, in his apartment in Concord. He worked as a salesman, wholesaling electronics."

Baldwin didn't need to work any more, judging from the figures I'd seen in Uncle Raleigh's probated will. "He's come up in the world, hasn't he? Any witnesses? To his being home in Concord?"

"I took his word for it. Didn't have any reason to doubt it. Do you?"

"Just a hunch."

"A hunch and a buck will get you a lottery ticket," Fleming declared. "You get lucky on either, you let me know."

Patricia Wong's house on Farragut Avenue was a small, pleasantly proportioned stucco, blue with white trim. It had a well-kept garden and it was obvious that Mrs. Wong did the keeping. I found her at the side of the house pruning an azalea, with a sedate black standard poodle for company. As I approached the house, the poodle got up from its spot on the grass and walked over to inspect me.

"He won't hurt you," Mrs. Wong said, with a friendly smile. She was in her early sixties, dressed in blue jeans and a blue work shirt. Today the sun shone and it was warmer than it had been earlier in the week. The poodle sniffed my shoes, legs and hand, then wagged its short tail to indicate I was okay. Mrs. Wong set down her pruning shears and removed her straw hat. I saw that she had shoulder-length black hair, streaked liberally with silver.

"My name is Jeri Howard," I told her. "I'm a private investigator. I'd like to ask you some questions about Raleigh Lambert."

The smile left her face, replaced by sadness in her large brown eyes. "Why?"

"Are you satisfied that his death was an accident?"

She didn't even stop to consider. Instead she shook her head resolutely. "Not at all. But he wouldn't have killed himself either."

Fifteen minutes later we were in Mrs. Wong's living room, seated on a rosewood sofa. She'd made tea, and the strong jasmine scent filled the air. The poodle stretched out at our feet and sighed with contentment.

"Tell me about Raleigh Lambert," I said.

Patricia Wong smiled. "Raleigh was the most charming

man. Dapper, handsome, debonair. I don't think I would be exaggerating if I compared him to Cary Grant or Fred Astaire. Not in looks, really. But he had that air about him. Let me show you a picture."

She stood and crossed the room to a shelf which held numerous framed photographs and returned with one, which she handed to me.

I examined it and grinned. I could see Lambert robbing a casino and romancing Grace Kelly in *To Catch A Thief*, or dancing with Cyd Charisse and total aplomb in *The Band Wagon*. He looked like a pistol, his long thoroughbred's face topped by a full head of white hair. Incredibly bright blue eyes smiled out from a tanned face. In this head-and-shoulders shot, Lambert wore a white shirt and I saw what looked like a tennis racquet propped on one shoulder.

"That was taken at the National Senior Games, five years ago," Mrs. Wong said. "Raleigh won gold medals in both singles and doubles. He was so alive. I just can't believe he'd take his own life. Nor can I believe he would be so careless as to lower the garage door before he'd turned off the engine."

"Where does that leave us?" I asked, not yet ready to say the word I'd been thinking ever since I saw that flicker of panic in Harold Baldwin's eyes when I'd mentioned dear uncle Raleigh. Murder?

Mrs. Wong wasn't ready to say it either. Instead she reached for her jasmine tea. "Why are you asking these questions?"

I decided I wouldn't tell her about that strange look in Harold Baldwin's eyes. At least not right now. "A week before he died, Raleigh Lambert left his Corvette at a repair shop in Oakland. He never picked it up."

"The Corvette," she mused. "I wondered what happened to it. Raleigh and I used to tool down Highway One in that

Corvette, playing the radio and singing along." She sighed. "Raleigh loved old cars. He stored most of them in Oakland, but he had several at the house. There was a T-Bird, a Packard. He even had an Edsel."

She looked as though she were having such a wonderful time reliving the past with Raleigh that I hated to bring her into the present. "Now the garage owner is trying to sell the Corvette. He does have a lien, because the repairs were never paid for. But he hasn't taken the legal steps that would enable him to sell the vehicle. A friend of mine is interested in buying the car, so I started checking into it. That's how I stumbled into this. I got curious about why no one ever claimed such a valuable car."

"Harold must not have known it was in the shop." Mrs. Wong freshened our tea. "I suppose now that he does, your friend will have to buy the Corvette from Harold instead of the garage owner. Harold got rid of all of the cars, except the Jaguar. I think he sold them to a museum or another collector." She sighed. "Harold couldn't wait to trade up from his green beat-up Honda and his one-bedroom apartment in Concord. He's let both the house and garden go to seed. He may have Raleigh's money, but he'll never have Raleigh's style."

"How long had you known Raleigh?"

"Over twenty years," she said. "He and my late husband both loved tennis. I knew his wife Felicia. She died a long time ago. When we were both widowed we started seeing more of each other. Raleigh and I talked about marriage but we decided we were quite happy just keeping company."

"How would your families have reacted to a marriage?"

"My children wouldn't have minded at all. In fact, my daughter used to ask me when Raleigh and I were going to elope. I think Harold was afraid I'd do just that and get his inheritance. Raleigh and Felicia never had any children, you see. Harold's mother was Raleigh's only sister."

I nodded. "Tell me about that night."

"We'd been to a ballroom dance contest at the Claremont. We won first place. I still have the trophy." She smiled fondly at his photograph. "Raleigh was the only man of my acquaintance who could tango. Does that sound like a man who would kill himself the same night?"

"No, it doesn't. But he did have liver cancer."

"I realize that. He told me the day he was diagnosed." Mrs. Wong sipped her tea. "You see, Felicia died of ovarian cancer. A very long and painful death. Raleigh told me he wouldn't go that way. I think he would have killed himself before he became totally incapacitated. But he wasn't. He'd only found out about the cancer a month before. He was going to try radiation and chemotherapy. He would have fought the disease hard before giving in to it."

"Had he been drinking that night?"

"Well, yes," she said, a tad reluctantly. "We both had. But he certainly wasn't drunk. Raleigh held his liquor like the gentleman he was. I didn't detect any sign of intoxication while we were driving home."

"What time did you get here?"

"About ten. He saw me to the door. I invited him in for a nightcap, but he declined. It was a Thursday night. Raleigh had a tennis match at nine Friday morning, and I was taking a class. Besides, I think we were both tired from all that dancing."

I had to agree with her that it didn't sound as though Lambert had killed himself. Maybe he was more intoxicated than she'd thought. "Who found the body?" I asked.

"Teo Martinez, Raleigh's doubles partner. When Raleigh didn't show up for their tennis match, Teo called and didn't get any answer. Finally he went by the house. He heard the car running in the garage as he walked up the driveway." Mrs. Wong shuddered. "Poor Teo."

"So there was no one there besides Raleigh. He didn't have a housekeeper?"

Patricia Wong shook her head. "No household help. He had a cleaning service that came in once a week, on Monday. And he liked to cook for himself."

When I drove into the parking lot of Musetta's repair shop the little red Corvette was gone. I went looking for Del, who glared at me from his grubby lair.

"You got some nerve showing your face around here, lady. I got a hotshot lawyer threatening to hand me over to the cops, charge me with conversion or some damn thing. All because you stuck your nose in." He stared glumly at the spot where the Corvette had been. "Why couldn't you have just bought it?"

"I wasn't really interested in buying the car, Musetta. I'm a private investigator. Besides, it's your own fault. You should have made more of an effort to contact the legal owner. Did you know Lambert?"

"Never met him till he brought that Corvette in here. He said his regular mechanic had retired, and he'd heard I did good work. Told me he collected cars and if I did a good job on the Corvette, maybe we'd have us a long-term arrangement."

"But a week later he was dead. You must have known that, must have seen the article in the *Tribune*." I waved away his protests. "You figured his heir wouldn't miss one car out of half a dozen. So you waited a couple of years before selling it. You should have gone to the DMV for an authorization for lien sale. But they might have tumbled to the fact that you hadn't made any effort to contact Lambert that the repairs were done. Or his heir."

"Swear to God, I did try," Musetta insisted. "I called three, four times. I left messages on his answering machine. I even went by the house twice."

"When?"

"A week after he left the car. I drove up to Piedmont one night after I closed the shop. Made another trip the very next morning, hoping I'd catch him before he left the house."

My ears pricked up. "What day of the week was that?"

Musetta sighed. "Lambert left the car here on a Friday. Only reason I remember that is I was planning to cut out early and go fishing. I told him I couldn't get to it until Monday. He said that was fine and to call him when it was ready. I finished the work late Monday afternoon. Called, left a message. Same thing the next three days. I start to wonder if the guy's out of town. Finally I went by the house, Thursday. I know it was Thursday, 'cause that's my bowling night."

Thursday was the night Lambert had squired Mrs. Wong to the dance contest at the Claremont. "Who did you talk with? What did you see?"

"Nothing," Musetta said. "There wasn't anyone home. Not even a maid, in a big house like that. I rang the doorbell. Zip. So I figured I'd swing by there Friday morning, before I came over here to open the shop."

So Musetta had been at the Sea View address again Friday morning, the same morning Lambert's body had been found by his friend Teo. "I want you to think very carefully," I told him. "About that Thursday evening when you went to Lambert's house. Were there any cars in the driveway?"

Musetta screwed up his face as he looked back three years. He nodded. "A couple, covered up. Couldn't tell what make they were. There was this beat-up Honda at the side of the garage. I figured it belonged to the household help. That's why I was surprised when no one answered the door. I thought . . ." He paused and looked confused. "I thought someone was there. That's it. I looked in the window when I rang the bell. Coulda sworn I saw someone in the house. But no one answered the door."

"Was the Honda there when you came back Friday morning?" Musetta hesitated. "Think. What time? You were on your way to the shop, so it must have been—" I broke off and looked at the hours listed on the repair shop's door. "You open at seven, so it must have been six-thirty, quarter to seven."

Musetta nodded. "Yeah, it was just getting light. I didn't go to the door. I sat in my car at the curb, where I could see the porch and the garage, till I saw someone come out. It wasn't Lambert, though."

No, it couldn't have been Raleigh Lambert. He was sitting behind the wheel of his '65 Mustang in that detached garage, dead from carbon monoxide poisoning. If Musetta had walked up the driveway he'd have heard the Mustang's engine. It was still running, as it had been all night, when Teo Martinez found the body later that morning. So whoever had left Lambert's house while Musetta was parked at the curb must have heard that car. Unless that person was deaf—or chose to ignore it.

I probed Musetta's memory enough to get an adequate description of the person he'd seen that morning. Then I went up to Piedmont.

Harold Baldwin didn't look any happier to see me this time than he had the last. While he stood at the door, I strolled past him, through the foyer to take a look at the living room. I didn't see any of the fine porcelain Raleigh Lambert was supposed to have collected. Maybe his nephew had sold it all, the way he had the classic cars.

He followed me into the room. "What are you doing here?"

"The little red Corvette. The one that was left at the garage."

"You wanted to buy it? My lawyer is taking care of it. If you still want to buy the car you can get in touch with him." He rattled off a name and phone number. I didn't bother to write it down.

"Such a shame about your uncle dying that way." Baldwin frowned at me. "I understand he killed himself."

"He had cancer," Baldwin said with a shrug. "My aunt died of cancer. I guess he just didn't want to go that way."

"So you knew it was coming. Still, it must have been quite a shock when you found him."

"I didn't find him. His doubles partner found him."

"So you weren't here at all, either Thursday or Friday."

"Of course not. I lived in Concord then. I was at home."

"Right. I suppose you sold that Mustang. Must have had all sorts of unpleasant connotations, what with Uncle Raleigh dying in it. You sold all his cars, except the Jag and the Corvette. But you didn't know about the Corvette. When did you unload the Honda?"

"What Honda?" That look was back, the one I'd seen in Baldwin's eyes the first time I mentioned his uncle and a car.

"According to Patricia Wong, you used to drive a little green Honda. After Raleigh's will was probated you couldn't wait to shed your one-bedroom apartment in Concord and your old car. She was right. You may have Raleigh's money but you sure as hell don't have his style."

"I don't know what you're talking about," Baldwin stuttered.

"Sure you do. You came out of the house, got into your beat-up Honda and drove off. But not before you checked the garage to make sure Raleigh was dead. You might have gotten away with it, if it hadn't been for that little red Corvette. Someone saw you that morning—the garage owner. He wanted to catch the owner. I guess he just did."

I picked up the phone and called Sergeant Fleming. "I got lucky," I told him. "And I'm not talking about the lottery."

"Voice Mail" is a new story. It came about as I listened to a series of voice mail messages, all on the same subject. Hearing those messages got me thinking about the way we communicate now, by e-mail, by voice mail, detached and at a distance, without the immediate feedback one receives in a face-to-face conversation, or even the voice-to-voice exchange of a telephone call. In this story, a woman uses voice mail to communicate her hostility to her soon-to-be ex-husband. He uses a different method of communication, and as you'll see, there's a reason for that.

Voice Mail

All right, asshole, where the hell are you?

You were supposed to pick up Brandon and Sara half an hour ago. No, make that forty-two minutes ago. You stood them up. *Again.*

That's the fourth time in five months. You'd better believe I'm keeping score. I'm writing it down. I've got a little list, just like the Lord High Executioner in *The Mikado*. I write it down, every time you lie to them, every time you cheat them by promising you'll spend time with them, and then just don't show up.

You say you want joint custody of the kids, because you love them so much. You say you can't bear to be apart from them. That's bullshit, and you know it. What makes you think you can take care of a six-year-old and an eight-year-old? Ego, of course. You lawyers have plenty of that, and you've got more than most. The only person you're interested in taking care of is yourself.

Right now Sara's in tears. She thinks you forgot about taking them to the beach house this weekend. Remember, the only reason I let you use the beach house at all is because the children love it so much. Sara doesn't realize that money is more important to you than her. Than anyone, or anything else. Brandon's trying to keep that stiff upper lip you're always talking about. The last time I looked, his lip was quiv-

89

ering. You and your macho bullshit.

You may be able to fool your partner, the sleazy divorce lawyer, and you may be able to put one over on that idiot judge—but not me. Not a chance, buster. It took awhile, but I got wise to you. You don't give a damn about these kids. You're just playing custody games to get back at me. And to get out of paying child support.

By the way, I had plans for this weekend, too, just in case you care. Which you don't.

Friday, 7:07 p.m.

Listen, jerk-face, if you're not here in fifteen minutes, you can forget about having the kids this weekend. Make that ten minutes. I don't care what it says about every other weekend in that so-called custody agreement your mouthpiece foisted on me.

And don't hand me that line about being busy at work, chasing ambulances, or padding your billable hours, or having to take one last phone call from one of your sleazy clients. If you want to see the children, you better stop making excuses and get over here. Now. And in the future, you get here on time, six o'clock, on the dot, just like it says in that damn agreement. Not that it's worth the paper it's printed on.

You bastard, I've had to cancel—What's that, Brandon? Daddy's car is at the end of the driveway? OK, asshole. You're off the hook this time. Just barely.

Sunday, 8:26 p.m.

What the hell are you trying to pull now? What do you mean, bringing the kids back so late? You were supposed to have them back here at six. Then you drive in at a quarter past eight. It's late, it's dark outside. So what do you do? You just open the door of your overpriced Mercedes and dump two little kids out at the end of the driveway, like they were a couple of sacks of trash. Gotta hand it to you. That's really being a responsible parent.

What's the matter, asshole? Are you scared you'll sully your trophy car if you pull into the driveway? Are you afraid to face me? You ought to be. Well, you're not getting off that easy. You won't talk to me. That's fine. I can leave voice mail messages until the cows come home. I can leave voice mail messages until the cows turn into hamburger. I can leave voice mail messages at all hours of the day or night, so that every time you pick up the phone you'll have to hear my voice. You'll have to listen to me, whether you want to or not.

Monday, 11:03 p.m.

You slug. You unregenerate, unmitigated, womanizing bastard.

This is a new low, even for you. Brandon and Sara finally told me about their weekend. You brought your latest bimbo to the beach house. They wanted to know why that lady Yvette was sleeping in Daddy's bedroom. Lady? Hah! No wonder you dropped the kids off after dark. Didn't want me to see the bitch.

For God's sake, show a little class.

Oh, that's right, you don't have any.

Well, class or no, here's some advice. Fuck your whore somewhere else. Not at the beach house with your kids in the next bedroom. Not where the children can see you. Or hear you. They're only six and eight. They don't need to see your slut running around half-naked, with her boobs hanging out.

91

Or listen to her squalling while you put it to her.

Still thinking with your prick. But when did you ever stop?

Yvette, huh. Sounds like a something a cheap hooker would call herself. Is that where you found this one? Walking the streets? Or was she lap dancing at some strip joint, like the last one?

Don't bother planning to use the beach house for another rendezvous with Yvette the bimbette. I'm having the locks changed.

Tuesday, 11:47 a.m.

You must be living in a dream world, even more than usual.

I got the latest missive from you, the big shot over-educated, full-of-himself lawyer, by way of your scum-sucking buddy who's also your divorce lawyer, who sent the package to my lawyer who sent it to me, via Ace Courier Service. You lawyers must own a piece of Ace Courier Service, the way you send everything by messenger.

Anyway, about this wad of toilet paper I received this morning. You call that a property settlement? I call it a work of speculative fiction. And not very well written at that. I give it an F minus.

A pair of so-called sharp lawyers like you and your mouth-piece shouldn't have to be told. But obviously you do need to hear it. So I'll tell you. Got a hot news flash for you, jerk. This is a community property state. I get half of everything. The house, the cars, the stocks, the bonds, every penny in all the bank accounts. And I want a big fat alimony check every month to go with all that child support you're going to pay to see your children through their education at the finest and most expensive colleges in the country.

I am taking you to the cleaners, asshole, and I hope you enjoy the ride. I know I will. And don't even think you're going to get away with hiding assets from me, buster. My lawyer is sharper than you and your lawyer put together. You hide anything, she'll find it. She just loves to go after lowlifes like you.

You can forget about the beach house. No way in hell are you getting so much as a coaster. It's mine. I bought it before we were married, with the money I got when my father died. The title is in my name. You can't have it. So just forget about it. It isn't negotiable.

And by the way, you can also forget that little trial balloon you floated about the kids coming to live with you part of the week. Joint custody? Are you on drugs? Or is your overblown, aggrandizing self-importance affecting your brain more than usual? I don't even want my children near you every other weekend, let alone part of every week. Especially when you're humping Yvette the bimbette in the bedroom—with the damn door open, so your children can see and hear.

So forget any changes to the current custody agreement, the one you're so fond of waving in my face. Never happen. Shoot that balloon right out of the sky, asshole. You'll get those kids over my dead body.

Wednesday, 10:43 a.m.

I got your message. So you can't pick up the telephone and call like other human beings? Oh, that's right, in your sick and deluded mind, you're several planes above the rest of us mortals. Unable to communicate in normal fashion. Unable to communicate, period.

Well, at least I get to see Russ on a regular basis. He's the guy from Ace Courier Service who delivers all these envelopes. Russ and I are getting to be good buddies. He's much better company than you ever were, and much better looking, too.

As to your latest directive, no, you can't have the kids this weekend. You're supposed to see the kids the first and third weekends of the month, from Friday at six p.m. till Sunday at six p.m. That's according to the custody agreement you foisted on me. Well, I don't much like that custody agreement. But I said I'd follow it. To the letter. So no changes, buster.

I don't care if all of a sudden your shrew of a mother decided to crawl out from whatever rock she's been living under this year. I have plans for this weekend, and they include Brandon and Sara. It just so happens that my brother and sister-in-law will be here and they want to see the children.

Thursday, 1:38 p.m.

My brother and sister-in-law aren't coming. And I'm sick. Picked up some flu bug. So you can see the kids this weekend.

But that means I get them next weekend. I want that in writing. Our lawyers agreed that any deviation from the custody agreement has to be in writing. *Before* you take them.

So type it up and get it over here, buster. Call old Russ at Ace Courier Service. I hope he charges you an arm and a leg to deliver it. And you damn well better pick up Brandon and Sara on time and have them back on time. Or else you'll hear from me.

We both know how much you love that.

Friday, 3:12 p.m.

All right, the lawyer brigade called Ace Courier and sent over something. Russ just delivered it. But it's another work of fiction about the property settlement. I already have lots of novels on my bookshelves and any one of them is certainly more entertaining than this.

Besides, you didn't send over what I wanted. Where is that statement saying I get the children next weekend?

Friday, 6:23 p.m.

If I hadn't been feeling so ill I would have kept the children here instead of letting you take them for the weekend. But I'll cut you some slack—this time. Get the document to me by Monday. No later than Monday.

Friday, 7:51 p.m.

Sara left her doll here. She's already called twice. I'll leave it on the porch swing so you can come and pick it up. She won't go to sleep without that doll, so make damn sure you come and get it. I'm going to bed. I feel awful . . . It's this damn flu. I had the flu couple of months ago . . . Guess it's back again . . . I don't understand it . . .

Sunday, 10:53 p.m.

Listen, you bastard. Your mother—the harpy—has no business telling the kids a bunch of lies about their coming to live with you part of the time. It's not going to happen. You see the children on the first and third weekends of every month. That's it. Zippo, nada, to anything else.

95

I don't want her feeding them a bunch of crap. I don't want her seeing the children ever again. Period. To hell with her and the broom she rode in on.

Monday, 10:46 a.m.

I told you I want it in writing. You had the kids last weekend so I get them this weekend. Better whip up something on the computer and send it to me. I want it by noon. If you think you can put one over on me because I was sick all weekend, you're even more delusional than usual.

Any deviation from the custody agreement, however slight, has to be in writing. My lawyer put it in, I agreed to it, and so did you and your lawyer. So get with it. If you don't get off the dime and do it I'm going to insist you have it notarized, too. Just to add another layer of complexity. So I expect Russ from Ace Courier Service on my doorstep by lunch time, with an envelope containing that statement. Be nice to see old Russ again. He and I are becoming such good friends.

Monday, 1:27 p.m.

Ace Courier Service just sent Russ over to deliver something and what do you know? I open the envelope and it's some fat legal document about the beach house. No statement about who gets the kids this weekend. What's the matter with you, you don't understand plain English? I want that statement. And you'll never get the beach house. Never. Don't bother trying.

Tuesday, 10:47 a.m.

My attorney's secretary called to see if I got the document

she sent over, some document she got from you. I slept in this morning. Sick again. Didn't hear the doorbell. Can't seem to shake this flu. The courier service didn't leave whatever it was. She said she'd send it out again this afternoon.

Tuesday, 2:56 p.m.

You bastard. You cold-hearted, manipulative bastard. Full custody of the children? You want full custody? You claim I can't take care of them properly? You claim I'm crazy? You claim I'm using drugs? You think you're going to force me to pee in a bottle so you can tell everyone I'm a druggie? When you know I've never tried anything but pot, and that was back in college. And you're the one who insisted I try it. You're the one who was snorting coke between classes, not me.

You miserable, lying, disgusting excuse for a human being. Don't you dare try to take my children away from me. I'll fight you tooth and nail.

Tuesday, 5:42 p.m.

I know why you're pulling the voice mail stunt. I thought about it and then I figured it out. I know what you're up to, Mr. Hotshot Lawyer who thinks his shit doesn't stink. And it's not going to work.

Oh, you thought you were being so clever. Make everyone think your ex-wife is crackers, completely nuts, so you can get custody of the kids. Tell everyone that I'm using drugs when all I've had is a touch of flu.

You play the martyr and complain to your divorce lawyer and anyone else who will listen that I'm crazy because I call you at all hours and leave voice mail messages.

Since when does that make me crazy? It's you who makes

me do it. You won't talk to me. You won't take my calls. You have your secretary say you're busy, so she can put me into voice mail. It's you who is forcing me to leave messages. You're doing it on purpose.

No, that doesn't mean I'm paranoid. It means I finally figured out your plan. It's so you'll have the voice mail messages.

I'll bet you save all those messages. I'll bet you record them on that little microcassette recorder you use to dictate letters to your secretary. I'll bet your poor underworked, underpaid, underappreciated secretary is going to be transcribing this message later today.

Hah! Hi, girlfriend! Whatever your name is this week. I'll bet you haven't been at the firm very long. You see, he goes through secretaries like someone with a cold goes through Kleenex. He's had three little victims already this year, and you're number four. The others quit as soon as they got his big self-important, abuse-the-help number. Bet that smarmy office manager didn't tell you that when you interviewed. Oh, no. You had to find it out from the people who really know— the guy in the mailroom and the other secretaries in the firm who refuse to work for him.

But I'm sure you've figured it out by now. Working for Mr. Lack-of-Personality isn't worth the lousy salary they pay you. Don't you just hate the tantrums he throws when things don't go his way? Don't forget all those long hours and the total lack of respect. But don't worry, honey. Whenever you get tired of wiping his butt there are other law firms in this city that pay a whole lot better and treat their employees like human beings.

Wednesday, 3:57 p.m.

Well, what do you know, asshole? A light bulb just went on over my curly head. You see, I paid a visit to see my lawyer this afternoon, to talk about your latest attack. Guess what? She's got a new secretary. Miss Brand New Secretary is quite a looker, if you like them on the skinny side, with big boobs. Which you do. Her name's Yvette. Isn't that just the funniest thing? And she wouldn't meet my eyes. I thought that was even funnier. I laughed my ass off.

Do you believe in coincidences, asshole? Well, neither do I.

Thursday, 11:12 a.m.

Hello, asshole. Just called to let you know I got that latest envelope you sent to my lawyer. You know, the one that my lawyer's new secretary—Yvette the bimbette—had sent over via Ace Courier Service. A nice big fat envelope, no doubt full of important legal documents in your campaign to try to screw me over one more time.

What a surprise.

I haven't opened it yet. I'm sure that's another surprise.

I'm on to you, asshole. You think you're going to put one over on me? Forget it. Not gonna happen.

You see, I had a nice long talk with Russ last night. He knocked on my door after dinner. You probably don't remember Russ. After all, he's just one of those little people you use and toss away. Well, not so little. He's a pretty big guy. Easy on the eyes, too. I've gotten to know Russ quite well over these past few months. Oh, you don't remember Russ? You should. I've mentioned him before.

Russ is the guy who works for the Ace Courier Service. That's the service you and Yvette the bimbette from my attorney's office use to send me all those envelopes. Lots of envelopes. Russ is over here sometimes two or three times a week. Or he was until lately.

You know what I do with all those envelopes? After I open them, I put them in the recycling bin in my office, like a good citizen. But you know, I haven't been feeling well, so I haven't emptied that recycling bin for a couple of weeks.

I can hear you saying, what the hell does this have to do with Russ? Well, Russ got fired from his job there at Ace Courier Service. You see, Russ had a little problem at work. It seems the people who run Ace bring a drug dog onto the premises every now and then. They want to make sure that their employees are not using illicit substances while on the job. Well, they had the drug dog in there Monday afternoon, right after Russ delivered an envelope here. It seems that drug dog alerted on Russ. There was cocaine on his clothes. Not much. Just a little bit. But a little bit is all it takes to get you into trouble, right? They fired Russ on the spot. Told him to clean out his locker and get out.

Now it's really odd that the dog should alert on Russ. He's a fine, upstanding young fellow—married, a kid on the way. He says he's never used the stuff. And he certainly wouldn't do anything that stupid, get himself fired when he's got a family to support.

So Russ got to thinking, trying to figure out where he'd been, where he might have picked up a trace of cocaine. Because that cocaine they found on his clothes, it was just a little trace, you know. Enough for the dog to pick up on, but barely enough for a human being to snort. It was just a little sprinkle, residue that might have sifted out of an envelope that's not sealed properly, or torn a little bit.

So Russ retraced his deliveries on Monday and wondered about the envelope he'd just delivered to me. And then last night he came over to see me. He and I started comparing notes. We went through that paper recycling bin and found the envelopes that Russ had delivered for the past couple of weeks.

And what do you know? There was this little bit of white powder in each of them. I'll bet some of that white powder sifted out of those envelopes every time I opened one of those damn envelopes. Bet some of it got into the carpet and the corners, on the furniture. I'll bet some of it's still there, because as you know, I'm not particularly regular when it comes to housecleaning.

You were going to call the cops, weren't you? Some time in the next week or so, right before the hearing on getting custody of the kids. You were going to call the cops and say you heard a rumor that your crazy ex-wife, the one who leaves you all those voice mail messages that you've been saving, is using cocaine and endangering your children. Somehow you'd engineer it so the cops would search the house. And of course they'd find that cocaine residue. And of course the judge would be shocked and horrified and give you custody of the kids, since it wouldn't be a good idea to leave them with a mother who's deranged and coked-up.

Except I'm not. And this little scheme you cooked up is going to blow up in your face.

Russ and I put those envelopes from the recycling bin in a big plastic bag. And this buddy of his from Ace Courier Service tipped him off that he'd picked up another envelope to be delivered to me.

So Russ was here this morning, waiting. And when that envelope got here, we didn't open it. We put it in a plastic bag. Then Russ and I took both of those bags over to a lab, to have all those envelopes tested. We told them to put a rush on it. So we'll have the results back in a day or so.

And if we find what I think we'll find, I won't see you in court, asshole. I'll see you in jail.

"Blue Eyes" appeared in the anthology Murder Most Feline. *I'm a cat person, so cats frequently appear in my novels and stories. One of them, in fact, looks a good deal like the cat in this story. Since I've worked in the legal field —and so has Jeri Howard, my series private eye—many of my ideas for stories involving Jeri have a legal hook. This story came about as the result of temp work for an attorney who specialized in wills and trusts. There was a provision in a will providing for the care of the decedent's pet. What could be simpler than that? Well, it's all in the way it's phrased, Jeri discovers.*

Blue Eyes

"Hey, Jeri," Cassie Taylor said with a chuckle. "Have I got a case for you."

I cradled the phone receiver between chin and shoulder as I switched off my computer, glancing at my watch. "I can give you half an hour. Then I've got to take Abigail to the vet."

Cassie's chuckle escalated into outright laughter.

"Why is it so funny that I have to take my cat to the vet?" I asked.

"It's not. Abigail, I mean. It's just that . . ." She stopped talking as she tried to get her laughter under control. "Come on over and I'll explain."

Mystified, I locked the door of J. Howard Investigations, located on the third floor of a building near Oakland's Chinatown. The front suite of offices is occupied by the law firm of Alwin, Taylor and Chao. Cassie's the middle partner. She and I have been friends since we were legal secretaries many years ago. Cassie went to law school, and I went into the private investigating business.

Cassie was in her office, dressed as usual in one of her spiffy lawyer suits. The elegant effect of the classy navy blue wool was spoiled somewhat by the fact that she'd removed her leather pumps and replaced them with a pair of battered running shoes, which were much more suitable for walking several blocks to the Alameda County Courthouse. At the moment, however, she was leaning back in her chair with her running shoes propped up on an open desk drawer, offering a

105

excellent view of her sleek legs.

With Cassie was her partner, Mike Chao. Short and stocky, he wore gray pinstripes, though he'd removed his jacket. The cuffs of his white shirt had been rolled up and he'd loosened the knot on his red tie. He was sitting in one of the two client chairs in front of Cassie's desk, holding a document in his hands. I sat down in the other client chair. "What's this case that has you in stitches?"

"I'm not in stitches, Cassie is," Mike said, looking glum. "Mainly because it's my problem and not hers. And I can't very well take it to court, because the judge will toss it back in my lap. It's about a cat. And a will."

"Don't tell me some little old lady died and left her estate to her cat Fluffy."

"Sort of," Mike said. "Only the cat's name is Ermengarde."

"Ermengarde! Who names a cat Ermengarde?" I shook my head. "That's cruel and unusual punishment."

"This from a woman named her cats Abigail and Black Bart," Cassie commented.

"Let me give you some background," Mike said. "My Aunt Mae had a friend named Sylvia Littlejohn. She was only in her early sixties. But she had cancer, and she died about ten days ago. She named Aunt Mae as executor of her will."

"I'm with you so far," I said. "When do we get to Ermengarde?"

Mike ran a hand through his straight black hair. "Mrs. Littlejohn gave Aunt Mae a sealed envelope containing her will and her funeral instructions. And she asked that Aunt Mae look after Ermengarde until the instructions in the will were carried out. So Aunt Mae's had the cat ever since Mrs. Littlejohn went into the hospital for the last time, which was the day before she died. The funeral was last week. Aunt Mae didn't open the envelope containing the will until after the service."

"So the problem is in carrying out the instructions in the will," I guessed.

"Exactly," Mike said. "As soon as Aunt Mae read the will she called me. For the most part, the document is fairly straightforward. Mrs. Littlejohn wasn't rich, but she was certainly well off. She left a number of substantial bequests to a number of friends as well as several charities."

"I take it one of these large sums was set aside for the care, feeding and upkeep of her cat Ermengarde," I said. Mike nodded.

"It's not worded that way, of course," Cassie chimed in. "The money is left to Mrs. Littlejohn's niece, for the specific purpose of Ermengarde's care, until such time as Ermengarde departs for that great cat tree in the sky."

"So Ermengarde's rich, or rather well off," I said. "Or her caretaker is. Unless the caretaker, or one of the other beneficiaries, decides to eliminate the cat."

Mike waved the document he was holding. "Mrs. Littlejohn anticipated that possibility, and took care of it. She states in her will that if the cat dies of anything other than natural causes, Ermengarde's bequest goes to several charities, not the caretaker or the other beneficiaries."

"And if the cat dies of natural causes?" I asked.

"The caretaker gets what's left," Cassie said.

"Aha." I digested this for a moment. "So what's the problem?"

"The problem's the niece. Or rather, the nieces. There are two of them."

I frowned. "Does the will specify which niece?"

"Nope," Cassie said.

Mike leafed through the pages until he found the

offending clause. "It says here that the money is bequeathed to Mrs. Littlejohn's niece, who will have full control of the money as long as it's spent to provide Ermengarde with all the comforts to which she's accustomed."

I reached for the will and read the clause, raising my eyebrows at the number of zeros after that dollar sign. "Wow. That's a lot of cat crunchies. Who the hell drew up this will anyway? A summer law clerk would have known better than to leave a beneficiary unnamed."

"For an attorney to make a mistake like that borders on legal malpractice," Cassie said, with a look that would have withered the yellow chrysanthemums on the credenza behind her desk.

I had to agree. I glanced through the rest of the will. Every other bequest specified a beneficiary by name, whether it was a person or an organization. The clause relating to Ermengarde was the only one that didn't.

It could have been a mistake. It was possible whoever typed the will had left out the name by accident. But if that was the case, the attorney—or Mrs. Littlejohn—should have caught the error when they proofread the will. Unless neither of them had read through the document. I looked at the date the will was signed. Earlier this year, ten months ago.

Somehow I didn't think the omission of the niece's name was a mistake. It smelled deliberate, not accidental.

"Aunt Mae says Mrs. Littlejohn's attorney was named Bruce Cathcart," Mike said. "She found his name and address on some other papers Mrs. Littlejohn left with her. Cathcart's also the one who notarized the will, as you'll see from the last page."

"But you can't find Cathcart," I finished.

"He's done a bunk," Cassie said. "Or so it appears. Which means we can't ask him just what he was thinking when he drafted up this will. If he was thinking at all."

"He's disappeared?" I asked.

"When I went looking for him," Mike said, "I couldn't find him. He rented an office in another law firm, Burke & Hare. When I contacted them, the office manager told me he'd left. And she claimed he didn't leave a forwarding address. But I got the feeling she wasn't telling me everything. All she would say was that he was there two years."

"What about before that?" I asked. "Was Cathcart associated with another firm? Did he have a partner?"

"According to the bar association, he was practicing solo when he rented space from Burke & Hare," Cassie said. "Before that, three years ago, he was with the Bestwick firm over in San Francisco. Nobody there will answer any questions about him. All the human resources manager will do is confirm that he worked there for five years. The bar association doesn't have a current address for him. Nor did they have any record of complaints against him. That doesn't mean there weren't any, of course, just that they didn't get reported to the bar."

"The guy definitely sounds like he's had some problems. If people don't want to talk about him, that could mean they have nothing good to say."

"That's what I thought," Mike said. "He must have had a secretary, though. If you could locate the secretary, maybe that would lead us to Cathcart."

"Worth a try," I said. "That's the first problem. I assume the nieces are the second problem. Only two so far?"

"So far," Mike said. "Aunt Mae organized the funeral according to the instructions Mrs. Littlejohn left, and she notified everyone in Mrs. Littlejohn's address book. She also put a notice in the *Oakland Tribune* and the *San Francisco Chronicle*. Both of the women showed up at the funeral, introduced themselves to Aunt Mae as Mrs. Littlejohn's nieces, and said they'd read the death notice in the *Chronicle*. Aunt Mae had never met either of them before. Neither had anyone else at the funeral. My aunt had heard Mrs. Littlejohn speak of a niece, but she was under the impression that they weren't close, and that the niece lived in another state."

"So you're not even sure the nieces are really nieces," I said. "Let alone the real niece."

"Their names are Cathy Wingate and Mary Hooper." Mike reached for a yellow legal pad on which he'd scribbled some notes. "Aunt Mae's got Mrs. Littlejohn's address book, and she says she didn't see either name there."

"And neither woman is listed as a beneficiary elsewhere in the will," Cassie added.

"Do they know about the will?"

Mike shook his head. "No. I thought it best not to bring up the matter until I was sure which one of them actually is Mrs. Littlejohn's niece. That's where you come in." He tore off a sheet of yellow paper. "Fortunately, Aunt Mae had the presence of mind to get their addresses."

I looked at the sheet. Both of Ermengarde's potential guardians lived in San Francisco. I asked Mike for his aunt's address and phone number, then I glanced at my watch, mindful of Abigail's vet appointment. As I stood up, I folded the paper and tucked it into my purse. "I'm on it. I'll get back to you as soon as I have anything."

"The sooner the better," Mike said. "I can't get this will admitted to probate until this mess is straightened out."

Abigail was not thrilled with the prospect of going to the vet. Neither of my cats are. They have been known to vanish at the rattle of a cat carrier latch. However, Abigail is old and fat, and I'm faster than she is. I scooped her up, ignoring the flailing paws and the outraged meows of protest, and wedged her through the door of the carrier. Then I strapped her into the passenger seat of my Toyota, and set off for Dr. Prentice's office, with Abigail muttering imprecations all the way.

Mike didn't know how old Ermengarde was, I thought, as I watched the vet examine Abigail. My own cat was nearing twelve, and I didn't want to think about losing her, but it was hard to know how long a cat would live, even the most pampered feline. Whether Ermengarde lived another year or ten years, she was going to live in style, considering the sum of money Mrs. Littlejohn had left for her care and feeding. And the niece who administered Ermengarde's money would also benefit quite nicely.

My vet conceded that Abigail had slimmed down some since our kitten Black Bart came to live with us. That had upped the cat's exercise level, plus I'd also been monitoring her diet. Dr. Prentice administered the required vaccines. That done, I opened the door of the cat carrier and Abigail retreated inside. Coming home from the vet was the only time she ever willingly got into the carrier.

"Do you by any chance have a client named Sylvia Littlejohn?" I asked Dr. Prentice. "With a cat named Ermengarde?"

"Yes, as a matter of fact, I do," the doctor said. "Why do you ask?"

"Mrs. Littlejohn died recently," I said.

"Oh, no," Dr. Prentice said. "I'm sorry to hear that. I hope someone's taking care of Ermengarde. She really loved that cat."

"Yes, the cat's being cared for," I said. "How old is Ermengarde? Is she in good health?"

"I'll have to check my records." Dr. Prentice left the

examining room and came back a moment later with a file. "Ermengarde's four. And she's in excellent health. If she doesn't have any major medical problems in the future, she could live another ten to twelve years."

I took my cat home, promising her that if she stayed healthy she wouldn't have to go to the vet again for another year. Then I headed over to an address in the Oakland hills to see Mike's aunt, who was caring for Ermengarde pending resolution of the mystery of her friend's will. I was eager to meet the newly rich cat.

She had blue eyes, slightly crossed. And there was a Siamese somewhere in her gene pool. She was small and elegant, with a luxuriant, long, fluffy coat, mostly white veering into pale champagne and dark brown in places. The dark patches on her dainty pointed face had the look of a harlequin's mask. Her ears and tail were tipped with brown, and so were three of her four paws.

Ermengarde was indeed a gorgeous cat. She gazed at me, unconcerned, with those big blue eyes, rested regally on a dark blue towel on Mae Chao's sofa. I held out my hand and let the cat take a delicate sniff. I knew I'd passed inspection when Ermengarde rubbed her pointy chin against my fingers, then allowed me to stroke her silky head.

I saw a white electrical cord running from under the towel to an outlet on the wall. "There's a heating pad under that towel," Mrs. Chao said. "Sylvia always had heating pads for this cat to sit on. She said cats are like heat-seeking missiles. They always find the warm spot."

I smiled, thinking of Abigail and Black Bart, and how fond they were of my down comforter, especially in winter. I'd have to try the heating pads for them.

I'd seen no other evidence of felines in residence, the sort of evidence I saw at my own house. Mrs. Chao's sofa, dark green with a floral motif of large pink peonies, showed no signs of cat claws shredding through the fabric. The beige carpet didn't have stray bits of cat food and kitty litter, at least none visible to my eyes. And I didn't see the usual buildup of cat hair anywhere else except the blue towel on which Ermengarde rested. That was covered with long white strands. Either Mae Chao wasn't a cat owner, or she was extraordinarily tidy and had extremely well-behaved cats. If there is such an animal.

"I take it you're not a cat person," I said. Mrs. Chao had made tea, and I sipped at the fragrant jasmine brew.

"Not really," she admitted. "Although I really like Ermengarde. She's such a sweet, good-natured kitty. And very well-mannered. Of course, she's been subdued since she came to live with me. I'm sure she misses Sylvia."

I looked at Ermengarde, wondering what dark secrets of feline misbehavior lurked behind those crossed blue eyes. "Ermengarde's an odd name for a cat."

"Sylvia named her after an old nanny who took care of her when she was child," Mrs. Chao said. "She said Ermengarde —the woman, not the cat—practically raised her and her sister after their mother died. Sylvia was about eight when that happened. Her sister was four or five. Their father was a wealthy businessman here in Oakland, and he traveled a lot. So Sylvia and her sister were frequently left alone, with the original Ermengarde, who was a German refugee. She came over here right before World War II."

"I wonder why the cat reminded her of the woman."

"Oh, she told me." Mrs. Chao reached over and ruffled the cat's fur. "The original Ermengarde had blue eyes that were slightly crossed. When Sylvia saw this little white kitten at the Oakland SPCA four years ago, she immediately thought of Ermengarde. Who has been dead for years, of course."

"What was the sister's name?"

"Oh, dear, let me think." Mrs. Chao reached for the cup of tea she'd set on the lamp table at her end of the sofa. "Lucille, that was it. And I believe her married name was Fanning. From the way Sylvia talked about her, I gathered that the sister was dead. And that they'd been estranged for many years."

That would explain why no one among Mrs. Littlejohn's contemporaries seemed to know that she'd had a niece, until the two women claiming kinship had shown up at the funeral.

I asked if I could look at Sylvia Littlejohn's address book, the one Mrs. Chao had used to notify people of the funeral. It was a worn leather volume that looked as though its owner had used it for many years. I leafed through the pages slowly, looking at the names listed, as well as for scribbles in the margins and bits of paper tucked into the pages. As Mike had said, neither of the purported nieces was listed in the address book.

Which struck me as odd. Presumably Mrs. Littlejohn really did have a niece. Why else would she have designated the niece as the person to look after Ermengarde?

Mrs. Chao interrupted my thoughts with a question of her own. "What happens if they're not really Sylvia's nieces?" She scratched Ermengarde behind the ears, and I heard a contented purr rumbling from the blue-eyed cat.

"I guess we'll have to figure that out when the time comes," I said. "It might be up to the probate judge."

"Well, if nobody else wants her, I'll take care of her," Mae Chao said. "I don't care about the money. But I'm getting to be quite fond of this cat."

★ ★ ★ ★ ★

The law firm of Burke & Hare, where Bruce Cathcart had rented an office, was located in a suite on an upper floor of a high rise near Lake Merritt. The whole building was lousy with lawyers. I was surprised the management company dealt with anyone who didn't have a *juris doctor*.

The office manager at Burke & Hare wasn't all that thrilled about discussing the missing perpetrator of Mrs. Littlejohn's will, at least not at first. But in my business all it usually takes is a little cajoling. In the end, she and the secretaries in the firm dished the dirt.

They hadn't liked Bruce Cathcart much. He was arrogant, they said, and treated the administrative staff as though they were talking pieces of furniture. The attorneys at Burke & Hare didn't care for him either. In fact, the office manager finally admitted Cathcart had been asked to leave. She wouldn't tell me exactly why, but something in the way she skated around the edge of it indicated that it was about money. Wasn't paying his bills, I guessed.

What about Cathcart's secretary? I asked. Which one? came the reply.

Cathcart had several secretaries. Several left, no doubt because of the way he treated them. Others he hired through staffing agencies, then fired before he was due to pay the agencies for their fee for finding the employee. After pulling that stunt several times, word got out and the staffing agencies refused to work with him anymore. So he'd resorted to ads in the local newspapers to find temps and part-timers, none of whom stayed for very long.

Except the last one. She'd worked with Cathcart for several months. And she'd registered on the view screen at Burke & Hare for reasons other than her job proficiency.

"They were having a thing," the office manager said. "It

was more than just a working relationship, if you know what I mean."

"Office romance?" She nodded. "What was her name? And do you remember what she looked like?"

"Kay Loomis. She was . . ." She stopped and thought for a moment. "Late twenties, medium height, dark hair, blue eyes."

I went back to my office and cruised several investigators' databases, looking for information on Bruce Cathcart and Kay Loomis, as well as the purported nieces, Cathy Wingate and Mary Hooper. Cathcart seemed to have vanished completely. A look at his credit report gave ample evidence why. The attorney's finances had gone down the tubes long before he took a powder.

Interestingly enough, Loomis had dropped out of sight about the same time Cathcart had. Maybe they'd run off to a desert island together. I quickly squelched that romantic notion. It was more likely they were in this scam together. I just had to figure out exactly what the scam entailed, and how they were pulling it off.

There wasn't much information on either Wingate or Hooper. It looked like they'd both surfaced in San Francisco earlier this year, just before Mrs. Littlejohn had signed that new will Cathcart drew up for her. And not long before the attorney disappeared. Wingate lived in Bernal Heights, Hooper in the Richmond District. When I dug further, I discovered that both women worked as secretaries, temping for one of the staffing agencies that specialized in legal support staff.

I had a late lunch at the nearby deli, then drove across the Bay Bridge to San Francisco. My first stop was in the city's Financial District, which was also lousy with lawyers. The firm of Bestwick, Martin & Smithson, where Cathcart had worked before hanging out his shingle in Oakland, occupied several floors in another highrise, on California Street.

I took the elevator to the Bestwick reception area and worked my way through a receptionist and an office manager before I found anyone with an axe to grind. She was an associate in Wills and Trusts. Her opinion of Bruce Cathcart was, in her words, lower than snail snot. But she really couldn't go into detail, not right here in the office. She told me to meet her downstairs in the lobby in fifteen minutes. It was more like twenty. We went outside, then across the street to one of the espresso joints that spring up in this part of town like weeds in a garden.

"The guy's a loser," Beth Fonseca told me, slugging down her cappuccino as though she needed a late afternoon infusion of caffeine. "I'm surprised they didn't fire his ass sooner."

"They fired him? Why?"

"Misconduct, negligence, misappropriation of funds. You name it."

I asked her to name it. She was reluctant at first, but I assured her that we'd never had this conversation. So she gave me a few examples of Cathcart's skullduggery, the kind that could get him disbarred or jailed.

After the attorney went back across California Street I finished my latte. Time to meet the nieces, I thought, glancing at my watch. It was late enough so that even if they'd worked that day, they should be home.

I retrieved my car and headed west in the thickening rush hour traffic. Mary Hooper lived near the intersection of Twenty-First Avenue and Lake Street. Finding a parking place anywhere in San Francisco is always a chore, and it took me several passes before I wedged my Toyota into a space between a fire hydrant and someone's driveway. The apartment was on the lower level of a house in the middle of the block, looking as though it had been converted from a garage.

I rang the bell. No answer.

I went back to my car and kept an eye on the place until I saw a gray Ford pull up outside the house. The driver was a man. The woman in the passenger seat leaned over and kissed him, then got out, walking toward the house. I jotted down the plate number as the Ford pulled away. By the time the woman entered the apartment I was out of my car and headed toward the house.

Definitely a converted garage, now a bare-bones studio, I thought, judging from what I could see when Mary Hooper opened the door. Late twenties, medium height, I thought, looking her over. Her dark brown hair fell to her shoulders, and she had blue eyes. Just like Kay Loomis, Cathcart's last secretary. Was that Cathcart in the Ford? I wondered.

I introduced myself, telling Mary Hooper that I worked for the attorney handling her aunt's will. "He's a little concerned about some irregularities," I said. "For instance, you're not named directly as a beneficiary. There's just a reference to a niece."

"I'm surprised she mentioned me in her will at all." She poured herself a glass of orange juice, then held the carton up and asked if I wanted some. I declined. She took a seat on the end of the futon on a frame that served as both bed and sofa, and crossed her legs.

"Mother and Aunt Sylvia weren't close. I don't know why, and now that Mother's dead, I can't ask her," she added regretfully. "When I moved here earlier this year, I decided to make contact. I wish I'd done it sooner. Aunt Sylvia was really a nice lady." She sipped her orange juice. "What's going to happen to her cat? She really doted on that cat. I'd be happy take it."

I looked at her face, trying to detect signs of duplicity. I saw none, only concern for Ermengarde's fate. "The cat's being cared for. How did you know she had a cat?"

"Oh, I was over at Aunt Sylvia's house a couple of times."

"It's interesting," I said, "that you weren't listed in her address book."

"Really? That's odd. Maybe she had my number written down someplace else."

"Maybe. It was lucky that you saw the notice of the funeral in the newspaper."

"Yeah, it was," she said, smiling again. "I would have hated to miss the service."

"And it would have made it more difficult for me to find you," I said, "if you hadn't given your name and address to Mrs. Chao. Then I had to wait until you came home. Were you at work?"

She nodded. "Yeah, it's just a temp job, in a law office. I'm doing that until I find a job I like."

"More job opportunities here than where you lived before?" I asked.

"Definitely more," she agreed. "There weren't as many jobs back home." She took another swallow of juice and smiled at me again.

"Where was that?"

Her smile grew less welcoming. "Detroit. That's where I grew up. Say, what is this, some kind of test?"

It was, but at this point I didn't know whether she'd passed or failed. I'd have to go back and do some more database research to see if her story about living in Detroit was true. And I wanted to put a trace on the license plate of that Ford that had dropped her off.

I took my leave. "You'll let me know about the cat," she

said. I assured her I would.

Cathy Wingate's apartment was on Cortland Avenue in Bernal Heights. When she opened her front door, somehow I wasn't surprised to see that she, too, matched the description of Kay Loomis. Late twenties and medium height, again, with blue eyes looking at me from a face fringed with short brunette hair.

I gave her the same spiel I'd given the other niece, and asked if I could come in.

"You mean Sylvia left me something?" she asked, amazed. "I'll be damned. What a sweet old gal." She held the door open wider. Her apartment was also a studio, sparsely furnished and with an air of impermanence. She looked tired, as though she'd had a rough day.

"I'm looking for a job," she volunteered, popping the top on a soda from her refrigerator. She asked if I wanted one, and I shook my head. She sat down on what looked like an old sofa bed and kicked off her shoes. "I had two interviews today. I'm bushed. It takes a lot out of you."

I went right to the questions. "What do you do?"

"Legal secretary, legal word processor. Whatever I can get that will pay the rent. At least for now." She sipped the coffee she'd poured for herself. "Both of my interviews today went really went well." She held up her hand and I saw that her fingers were crossed. "Wish me luck."

"Better job prospects here than in . . ."

"Denver," she said. "I moved here from Denver, not quite a year ago. I don't know about job prospects, but the weather is sure as hell better. So, what did Sylvia leave me? I don't mean to sound greedy or anything, but at this point, an extra fifty bucks would be a godsend."

"We'll get to that. Is your family still in Denver?"

She frowned. "Why all the questions?"

"I'm just curious about why Mrs. Littlejohn would leave you something in her will."

"Well, so am I," she said with a shrug. "I mean, I'm her niece. But it's not like we were close. I never even met her till I came out here. I decided since she was in Oakland I'd look her up."

"Why weren't you close?"

"She and my mom had a falling out, years ago. Mom didn't like to talk about it. And Mom's dead now, so I can't ask her."

"What about your father?"

"He's dead, too."

"What was his name?"

"George Cooper."

I digested this. Funny how Cooper and Loomis both had double Os. And it was a short walk from Cathy to Kay.

The phone rang. She made no move to answer it, instead letting her answering machine pick up the call. It was a man's voice. He didn't leave his name, just, "Hi, call me when you get in."

"Boyfriend?" I asked. Bruce Cathcart? I wondered, but I didn't say anything.

"Just a guy I've been out with a couple of times." Cathy Wingate set her soda on an end table and gave me a hard look. "I get the feeling you don't think I'm Sylvia's niece."

"Just exercising a little caution," I said, leaning back in my chair.

"If it will make you feel any better, I've got some old pictures that belonged to my mother. They show her and Sylvia when they were kids."

"I'd love to see them," I told her.

She got up and moved over to a desk that had been pushed against a wall. She opened a drawer and then walked back

121

toward me, opening the flap on a large accordion folder. She rummaged in one of the pockets and drew out a handful of snapshots. She sifted through the photos in her hand, then held one out to me. "Here. That's Mom on the left and Sylvia on the right."

I glanced at the photo, a faded color snapshot showing two youngsters in frilly dresses who could have been anyone's kids. "Did you know your aunt had a cat?" I asked.

"Oh, my God," she said, concern written on her face. "I forgot about her. Is somebody taking care of her? I should have asked that Mrs. Chao I met at the funeral. Sylvia loved Ermengarde. Did you know she named that cat after her old nanny? I knew why, too, the minute I saw the cat."

"Why is that?"

She handed me another photograph, this one a larger reproduction showing the two little girls standing on either side of a seated woman in a dowdy black dress. Cathy Wingate pointed at the woman's worn round face. "Ermengarde and the cat have the same eyes."

I looked at the photo and smiled. The woman's eyes, like those of her namesake, were blue, slightly crossed.

"But Aunt Mae said she thought Lucille married a guy named Fanning," Mike said. "You're telling me Cathy Wingate's father was George Cooper."

"Lucille's first husband was Tom Fanning. In fact, that's why Sylvia and Lucille had their falling-out. Tom was courting Sylvia, then changed his mind and went after her younger sister. After he was killed in a car accident, Lucille married George and they had one child, Cathy. She was in Sylvia's address book, by the way. As Mary Catherine Cooper, instead of her married name, Wingate. Sylvia never bothered to change the name."

"What happened to Mr. Wingate?" Cassie asked.

"He died of cancer last year, which is one reason Cathy decided to leave Denver for California. At the same time, Sylvia knew she was dying and wanted to make arrangements for Ermengarde. That's when she went to see Cathcart."

I smiled, this time with grim satisfaction. "I traced Cathcart from the plate number of that Ford. He was living in the Sunset District, as John Benson, a deceased client whose social security number he'd appropriated for new identification. Now that both Cathcart and Loomis have been arrested and charged, Kay's singing long and loud. Says it was all Bruce's idea. Turns out Sylvia did specify her niece Mary Catherine Cooper as Ermengarde's caretaker. After she'd signed the will, he substituted the altered page, then set up Kay in the role of the niece, Mary Hooper. What tripped them up was Ermengarde. Cathcart knew what the cat's name was. But he didn't know why Sylvia chose that name."

"So Mike gets the probate judge to sign off on your affidavit," Cassie said. "Cathy Wingate gets designated as Mrs. Littlejohn's one and only niece. And Ermengarde gets a home."

"Well, there's just one problem," Mike said, frowning. "And I don't think Jeri can fix it. Cathy Wingate's allergic to cats."

"Mrs. Lincoln's Dilemma" appeared in the anthology The First Lady Murders. *Mary Todd Lincoln was often vilified —wrongly, I believe—by historians. I've even heard her described as "the crazy one." When I dug into the historical record, I found the Mary who suffered the loss of three of her four children to disease, and the assassination of a beloved husband, shot before her eyes. Who wouldn't become unhinged by those blows to the spirit? I also found the Mary who was a fascinating person in her own right, an intelligent, vivacious and shrewd political wife who advised her husband on many occasions. It wasn't difficult to imagine her—and the associates who go places she can't—solving a mystery in Civil War–era Washington.*

Mrs. Lincoln's Dilemma

The soft yellow glow of the lamplight turned Mrs. Lincoln's white silk gown to a mellow cream color. The light also hid the shadows and the tiny wrinkles on her face as well. She vowed it took ten years off her age.

Her blue eyes sparkled. Tonight she wore pearls in her ears and at her throat, and several white camellias pinned in her light-brown hair. As she moved among the guests gathered in the East Room of the White House that evening in November of 1861, smiling and nodding, she felt as though she were still the Lexington belle who, with wit and vivacity, charmed her way through Springfield, Illinois over twenty years ago. Back then she'd caught the eye of many young bachelors, including a tall gangling lawyer named Abraham Lincoln.

Mrs. Lincoln swept regally past a cluster of cabinet wives. All of them, to her critical eyes, looked drab and dowdy. The Washington wags criticized her constantly, on everything from her involvement in politics to her extravagance and her manner of dressing. How dare a woman of Mrs. Lincoln's age bare her shoulders and décolletage, they clucked like a chicken house full of old hens. How dare she wear white, which was considered suitable only for a young woman.

She'd been told they called her "The Illinois Reine" because of her fashionable and lavish dress. Well, let them talk. The First Lady of the United States should look as elegant as General McClellan over there, resplendent as a peacock in his dress uniform.

She knew the gossip about her extravagance stemmed from her efforts to redecorate the White House. It was true she'd gone through the allowance set aside for refurbishing the residence. Unfortunately, the expenditures had come at a time when everyone was insisting that every last penny go into the war effort.

But the White House had been downright dilapidated when she, Mr. Lincoln and their boys had moved in. She'd been appalled at the sight of peeling wallpaper and broken furniture in every room. And the state dining room in the west wing had more broken china than whole. Why, the place had looked like a tawdry boardinghouse. She'd soon remedied that, at the cost of a good deal of money, and even more talk.

Mr. Lincoln is President, she told herself. He must have a suitable place to live. How much nicer the East Room looked with the new damask curtains and the fine carpet that replaced the threadbare rag damaged by the Frontier Guard, who would practice presenting arms right here.

As for politics, she was a politician's wife, and had been for nineteen years. She'd been interested in politics since those early years in Springfield, even before she'd married Mr. Lincoln and began keeping house and raising children. Her husband had asked her counsel many times throughout their marriage, and she'd readily given it. Why should she stop now, just to suit a bunch of pinched-nose critics?

She paused to speak with Secretary of the Treasury Salmon Chase and his red-headed daughter Kate, then moved on to a group of stiff-backed Army officers and their ladies. She felt a hint of coolness as they greeted her, and she knew why.

Her half-brothers, Sam, David and Aleck, had joined the Confederate Army after Fort Sumter. Her half-sister Emilie's husband was Confederate General Benjamin Hardin Helm. These younger siblings were Kentuckians, and their southern sympathies were to be expected. Despite the pain their allegiances caused her, Mrs. Lincoln felt a good deal of affection for the children born of Robert Todd's second marriage. Her stepmother was another matter. Mrs. Lincoln had left Lexington for Springfield just to get away from the hated Betsey Humphreys Todd.

She pushed away the image of her divided family, an echo of the now-divided nation. Her eyes searched for someone she had invited to the White House soiree, an old friend from Springfield who was in Washington on family business. On the other side of the room she spied Ada Belford, in a brown watered silk dress decorated with jet beads. Her gloved hand rested on the arm of a slender young man whose straight brown hair tumbled onto his forehead. When Mrs. Belford caught the First Lady's eye, she waved.

Mrs. Lincoln sidestepped a cavalry officer with a dangling sword and headed toward her friend. She passed just behind two men, civilians both, one tall and dark, with a hawk-like profile. The other was short and broad, with a head of ginger hair that went with his florid complexion. Their heads were bent together and they talked in low tones, as though they did not wish to be overheard. It was reasonable to assume they would not, given the crowded hubbub of the room. But Mrs. Lincoln heard a few words anyway.

"Shortage of woolens, as you well know," the tall man said. His voice was deep and flavored with a New England accent. ". . . play our cards right . . . could all be rich."

His companion nodded in agreement as he spoke, his voice a harsh whisper. "Depends . . . make it worth my while."

Mrs. Lincoln's route carried her away from their muted

words. Her lips thinned with disapproval as she drew her own conclusions about what she'd just heard. Speculators, out to make a quick killing in business while others were killed on the battlefields. They talked of getting rich, as though the war was nothing but a business opportunity.

She knew of the shortage of woolens for military uniforms. Mr. Lincoln had mentioned it over breakfast a few days ago. Only yesterday she'd heard with her own ears evidence of such a scarcity. As was her custom, she'd spent some time at one of the many military hospitals in the capitol, talking with a young Union soldier who seemed barely older than her own dear Willie. The soldier's leg had been amputated. Now that autumn was giving way to winter, he said, it was cold out on the battlefields and in the camps. The boy told her he and his compatriots often shivered for lack of adequate clothing.

The government, according to Mr. Lincoln, planned to remedy that problem by purchasing cloth from abroad. However, he added, such a move was sure to raise the ire of American manufacturers.

Her mouth curved back into a smile as she greeted Ada Belford with an embrace. "Ada, my dear. I'm so glad to see you."

Mrs. Belford took the First Lady's hand and squeezed it. "Mary . . . Oh, should I call you Mrs. Lincoln?"

"You've called me Mary for years. I see no reason to change now."

"Back in Springfield you weren't the President's wife," Mrs. Belford said. "It's good to see you again. Thank you so much for inviting us to your soiree."

"When I received your letter advising me that you were in Washington, I said to Mr. Lincoln that of course you must come. You and Edward both."

Edward Belford was a good-looking lad, if somewhat

solemn and studious, who had just turned eighteen. He resembled his late father, who had served in the Illinois legislature with Mr. Lincoln. And there was something, not just the name, but in the shape of his face and his eyes, that reminded Mrs. Lincoln of her own son Eddie, who had died eleven years earlier.

"Ada, your note said you are in town for your niece's wedding. A happy occasion."

Mrs. Belford nodded. "Happy, yet somewhat tempered by the course of this wretched war. Rachel is the daughter of my eldest sister, Olivia Hopkins. Her husband, Colonel Hopkins, was killed this past summer at Bull Run."

"A terrible tragedy," Mrs. Lincoln murmured. The war. It permeated everything. She'd never met Olivia Hopkins but she could imagine the horrible loss of a husband. Hadn't she herself experienced the loss of a child?

"Rachel's beau is an Army officer," Mrs. Belford continued. "He's posted here in Washington, but she fears he'll be sent elsewhere after the new year. If it weren't war time perhaps the girl could be persuaded to wait until spring for her wedding. But she's quite insistent on getting married as soon as possible. Young people these days . . ."

Difficult days, the First Lady thought. She and Mr. Lincoln had courted for nearly four years before their marriage, but these were different times. She understood the young woman's haste. A father already killed by this war, the unspoken fear that her sweetheart might meet the same fate.

Edward stood quietly as his mother regaled her friend with news of people back in Springfield. Then Ada Belford stopped and glanced over Mrs. Lincoln's shoulder.

"I hope you don't think I presumed on your invitation, Mary, but I brought my sister Ella and her husband, who are also here for the wedding. Allow me to present them. Mr. and

Mrs. John Grayson of Fall River, Massachusetts."

Mrs. Lincoln turned to her right and inclined her head to Ella Grayson, a pretty blond in a stylish blue dress. She was some years younger than her sister, and gave the impression of being quite giddy. Then Mrs. Lincoln glanced up, startled to find herself face-to-face with the tall hawk-faced man she'd overheard earlier, discussing the economic opportunities afforded by the shortage of woolens. She masked her surprise as Mrs. Belford continued her introduction. "Mr. Grayson owns a factory in Fall River."

"Indeed," Mrs. Lincoln said, turning on him her most dazzling smile. "And what do you manufacture, Mr. Grayson?"

"Woolen cloth, ma'am," he told her. "To be made into uniforms for the Army."

"You have a government contract, then." In the next few moments Mrs. Lincoln endeavored to find out more about Grayson's enterprise. But he was now quite close with his tongue, closer than he had been earlier with the red-haired man. He took his wife's arm and bowed to the First Lady, then to his sister-in-law. "Will you excuse us? There is someone I wish Ella to meet."

When the Graysons had moved away, Ada Belford sent Edward to fetch her a cup of punch. Then she leaned close to Mary Lincoln. "Have you had a chance to consider the matter I proposed in my letter?"

Mrs. Lincoln nodded. Ada Belford had an older daughter, married and living in Ohio. Edward was her only son, and since her husband's death two years earlier she'd been reluctant to let the boy out of her sight. He wanted to join the Army, had ever since Fort Sumter. It wasn't unusual. In fact, boys far younger than Edward were with the troops on both sides of the fight.

But Ada couldn't bear the thought of losing him. So she'd written to her old friend Mary, to ask a favor. Surely Mrs. Lincoln could arrange for a government job, any government job. Surely he could contribute to the war effort that way, and avoid any criticism for not being in the Army.

Mrs. Lincoln was certainly sympathetic to her friend's feelings. Her own son Robert, the eldest of the three surviving Lincoln boys, wasn't in the Army either, and the old hens were clucking about that, too.

Mary Lincoln was certainly no stranger to patronage. Ever since Mr. Lincoln had become active in politics, people frequently asked the politician's wife for favors. She was shrewd about how she granted them.

And how she went about obtaining them. She had examined the guest list for this evening's reception and noted that the Secretary of War's party included Major Charles Markham, whom she'd met before, at a reception given by the Chases. The major worked in the War Department, procuring supplies, he said, as he complained of a shortage of clerks. Surely he could use the talents of an intelligent young man like Edward Belford.

When Secretary of War Edwin Stanton had arrived, Mrs. Lincoln sent Henry Wilder in search of Major Markham. Henry was a clerk on the White House staff, and since he was from Illinois, Mrs. Lincoln had made him her unofficial assistant. She frequently relied on his discretion and efficiency.

Once summoned by Henry, Major Markham readily agreed to interview young Mr. Belford. "How can I refuse the First Lady?" he told her with a charming smile, as he bent low over her hand. "I'm sure I can find some employment for the young man."

Now Mrs. Lincoln lowered her voice and moved closer to Ada Belford. "I've already acted on your request. Edward has an appointment tomorrow with Major Markham, with whom I spoke earlier this evening."

She glanced about the room, seeking the major. Her eyes rested for a moment on the Secretary of War, but she didn't see Markham. Ah, there he was. Now, that was interesting. The major was talking with the red-haired man she'd seen earlier, with John Grayson.

By now Edward had returned with a cup of punch, which he handed to his mother. He listened politely as Mrs. Belford told him excitedly of his appointment with Major Markham.

"That tall officer there," Mrs. Lincoln said. "The one with yellow hair. He'll expect you at noon, at the War Department. Now, I want you to report back to me about your interview with the major. I'll be visiting one of the military hospitals tomorrow afternoon, the one near Union Station."

Mrs. Lincoln left the Belfords and moved around the East Room, pausing several times to speak with guests. Finally she joined her husband. At six feet four inches, to her own five feet two, he towered over her. Abraham Lincoln, the sixteenth president of the United States, looked down at his wife, in her billowing white silk, and smiled fondly. Then he leaned over and whispered in her ear. "You're as pretty as the day I met you."

Later, as the guests were leaving, Mrs. Lincoln caught Henry Wilder's eye. She pointed out the red-haired man, who trailed behind Secretary Chase's party. "Find out who he is," she directed the young man. Henry nodded and moved away. After all the guests had departed, Henry returned and made his report.

"The gentleman is named Simon Chester," he told her. "He's a businessman from New York. He was here as a guest of the senator from that state."

Mrs. Lincoln thanked him. She thought no more about

the red-headed man until the next day, when events gave her reason to do so.

Henry and two large troopers of the Frontier Guard escorted her to the hospital that rainy afternoon. She could hear the train whistles from the nearby railroad station as she read to a wounded soldier. When it was time to leave, Henry and the troopers walked with her down a corridor to the hospital's front door. There she saw Edward Belford, who had just entered. He looked so young and slender, in contrast with the bearded, burly soldier who followed a few steps behind him.

Henry and the troopers withdrew a few paces to allow her some privacy during her conversation with Edward. "How did it go, your interview with Major Markham?" she asked, pulling on her gloves. "Has he a place for you at the War Department?"

Edward Belford looked down at his muddy shoes and the damp cuffs of his trousers which gave evidence of a long walk in rainy weather. His eyes came up, meeting those of the First Lady.

"Mrs. Lincoln," he said slowly, "I kept my appointment with the major, but I told him . . . I mean, I appreciate all the trouble you've gone to but—"

"You're going to join the Army anyway," she finished, her voice quiet.

Edward ducked his head in quick assent. "Yes, ma'am. I want to serve my country and help Mr. Lincoln preserve the union."

"Those are admirable sentiments, Edward. I can't argue with them. Not here, anyway." She looked around her at the bustling hospital, so full of other young men who wanted to help her husband preserve the union. "Your mother will be upset."

"Yes, ma'am, I know. But I've made up my mind. I thought about waiting until after my cousin's wedding, but . . . well, I've waited long enough. I'll tell Mother this afternoon, as soon as I . . . well, there's somewhere I need to go first, but I'll tell her as soon as go back to Aunt Olivia's house."

"Good luck," she said, holding out her hand to the boy. "And God be with you."

He hesitated. "Mrs. Lincoln, there's something . . . well, I don't know who to tell. But I saw something that's odd."

"What's that, Edward?"

He lowered his voice. "After I spoke with Major Markham, I got lost in the War Department building. It's mighty big, and I got turned around. Finally I found my way out of the building. And who should I see outside, but my uncle John, the one that owns the mill in Fall River. I was real surprised to see him there. He was standing to one side as though he didn't want anyone to see him. But I guess he was meeting someone, because of what happened next."

"Someone joined him?" Mrs. Lincoln asked.

"Major Markham. Well, I didn't think that was odd, at least not at first, because Uncle John's got a government contract. He sells all his cloth to the Army, for uniforms. Then I got to wondering. If my uncle was there to see the major on business, why didn't they meet in the major's office?"

Why, indeed? the First Lady thought.

"So I followed them," Edward continued. "They went to a tavern, a few streets away. They met a man there, a ginger-haired fellow. He was at your reception last evening. I saw Uncle John talking with him there as well. And the major too."

"You're very observant, Edward. Did you go into the tavern? Could you hear what they were talking about?"

"I went inside, ma'am. But I couldn't hear what they were talking about. They had a drink together." The boy leaned closer to her. "Then Uncle John pulled out a wad of greenbacks. He gave a fistful to the major, and another to the other fellow."

"Good heavens." Mrs. Lincoln's suspicions were growing, particularly as she recalled that scrap of conversation she'd overheard last night. "They didn't see you?"

"I don't think so, ma'am. I left that tavern quick, I can tell you, and walked over here to meet you. I thought about it all the way over here. That's why I was late. Guess I was walking a bit slow." Edward frowned. "I hope I've done the right thing telling you all this. You have enough to worry about, Mother says."

Mrs. Lincoln laid her hand on his shoulder. "Yes, I'm glad you told me, Edward. Now, I'm expected at a meeting. As for the Army, you do what you must, and take care of yourself."

She stood and watched as the young man left the hospital, his shoulders back and his stride brisk and almost military. Then her view of Edward Belford was blocked as the burly man she'd seen earlier, an orderly, she guessed, headed quickly out the door.

Once outside in her carriage, Mrs. Lincoln turned to Henry. "I have an errand for you. I need more information on Mr. Chester, the red-haired man from last night. You said he was a businessman from New York City. See if you can find out more about him, especially what business he is engaged in."

She spent the next hour or so meeting with the redoubtable Miss Dorothea Dix, who was superintendent of Union Army nurses, and Miss Clara Barton, a volunteer who was working with the wounded, discussing how to improve hospital conditions. Then Mrs. Lincoln returned to the White

House. The President was still at the Capitol. Tad and Willie were being rambunctious, trying their mother's patience. She admonished the boys and went upstairs to take a nap. An hour later Henry Wilder knocked on the door. She admitted him and sent for tea.

"Mr. Chester, it appears, is an agent who represents cloth manufacturers," Henry said.

"Then there's nothing unusual about his speaking with Mr. Grayson," Mrs. Lincoln said in a low voice. "For Mr. Grayson makes cloth. Still . . ." she couldn't forget what young Edward had said about seeing Chester and his uncle with Major Markham in that tavern. Money changing hands, the boy said. Grayson's money. Surely that was not on the up and up.

Her train of thought was derailed by the approach of another member of the White House staff bearing not tea, but a note. "From a Mrs. Hopkins," the man said. "It just arrived, and the messenger who delivered it said it was urgent."

Mrs. Lincoln took the envelope and turned it over in her hands. She recognized neither the handwriting, nor the name. No, wait, Hopkins. Wasn't that Ada Belford's sister, the colonel's widow? She opened the envelope and pulled out a single sheet of paper. As she read the words written on it, her mouth opened in a shocked gasp.

"Mrs. Lincoln?" Henry asked, his own face worried. "What is it?"

"A carriage, Henry," she said in a choked voice. "Call for a carriage, and quickly."

Mrs. Hopkins lived in a modest house on Third Street, near East Capitol Avenue. It seemed to take forever to get there. Olivia Hopkins, a gaunt-faced woman in black, greeted Mrs. Lincoln and Henry Wilder at the door.

"Thank you so much for coming, Mrs. Lincoln. It means so much to Ada. She's simply prostrate with grief, ever since the policeman arrived to tell us the news."

"This is dreadful," the First Lady said. "May I see her now?"

"Of course. She's been asking for you."

The Frontier Guard troopers who had come with Mrs. Lincoln and Henry took up a position in the vestibule, while Henry waited in the parlor. Mrs. Lincoln followed Mrs. Hopkins up the stairs. "Tell me what happened."

"I know little, other than what the policeman told me, when he arrived here late this afternoon." Olivia Hopkins paused at the landing, one knobby hand on the banister. "Edward was found in an alley off Fourteenth Street. He'd been stabbed." Mrs. Hopkins shuddered, then her faced hardened as she went on. "Waylaid by some ruffian, the policeman said, and killed for the contents of his pockets."

"I saw him at one of the military hospitals this afternoon," Mrs. Lincoln said. "The one near Union Station. That's just north of here. He was coming back here to your house afterwards, he said." She stopped and shook her head. "No, wait, he said something about having someplace to go. Where on Fourteenth Street was he found?"

"Not far from Pennsylvania," Mrs. Hopkins said, continuing upstairs.

"He was near the White House, then," Mrs. Lincoln said, half to herself. Where had young Edward Belford gone after he left the hospital? It was simply too convenient that he should be dead this rainy evening, a few short hours after he'd told her of what he had seen in that tavern.

When they reached the upper floor, Mrs. Hopkins led the way to a door at the rear of the narrow house, and opened it. She stepped to one side and let Mrs. Lincoln enter, then qui-

139

etly closed the door, leaving the two women from Springfield alone. Mrs. Lincoln had tried to prepare herself for this moment, on the way here from the White House. Yet it was not enough. Never would she forget the sight of Ada Belford's tear-ravaged face.

Much later she came wearily down the stairs, where Henry and the two troopers waited. In the parlor Olivia Hopkins poured tea. The handsome young woman with her, Mrs. Lincoln had already guessed, was Rachel Hopkins, the one who was to be married.

As Rachel handed tea to Henry and the troopers, Mrs. Hopkins offered a cup and saucer to Mrs. Lincoln. "How is she?"

"Asleep," the First Lady said, taking a seat. "She cried herself to sleep."

"Good. She needs rest." Mrs. Hopkins sighed. "I know. I've been through it. My husband was killed last summer." She stopped and her eyes moved to a portrait of a military officer hanging above the mantel.

"Ada told me of your loss," Mrs. Lincoln said. "I am sorry."

"He was a military man." Mrs. Hopkins's face regained the steely composure she had shown earlier. "A military wife expects casualties, or she has no business marrying into the Army. But the loss of a child, no matter his age, is hard."

"I know." As Mrs. Lincoln raised the teacup to her lips, it was not Edward Belford's face she saw, but Eddie Lincoln's, dead these eleven years.

Rachel joined the two older women. "I'm sorry I wasn't here when the policeman came," she told her mother. Then she glanced at the First Lady, and explained further. "I spent the afternoon with my friend Daisy Markham, shopping for my trousseau."

"Markham?" Mrs. Lincoln, bone tired a moment before, found herself revived, not by the tea, but by the mention of the familiar name.

"My dearest friend from school," Rachel told her. "She's married to an Army officer."

"Major Charles Markham of the War Department?" The First Lady carefully set the teacup in its saucer. "He was at a reception Mr. Lincoln and I gave at the White House."

Rachel nodded. "I only know him through Daisy. But I believe he's acquainted with Uncle John."

He is indeed, Mrs. Lincoln thought. Intimately.

"Speaking of your Uncle John and Aunt Ella . . ." Mrs. Hopkins consulted the clock on the mantel and frowned. "I've sent word to them at the same time I sent that note to Mrs. Lincoln. I thought they'd be here by now."

"They're not staying here?" Mrs. Lincoln asked.

"Dear me, no," Olivia Hopkins said, her voice tart. "I haven't the room. Nor is my simple little house enough to satisfy my brother-in-law's pretensions. He's an ambitious man, who thinks himself quite above the rest of us. No, they're staying at Willard's Hotel."

Willard's? Mrs. Lincoln sipped tea, then straightened. Willard's Hotel was located at Fourteenth Street and Pennsylvania Avenue. Had Edward gone to see his uncle this afternoon, to confront him with what he'd seen earlier?

The doorbell sounded, and Rachel went to answer it. The Graysons had arrived. Mrs. Lincoln greeted them politely, her eyes moving from Mrs. Grayson's round pretty face and expensive clothing to her husband's shrewd dark visage. Suddenly she found that she didn't want to be in the same room as the man. She glanced at the clock, then set the cup aside.

"I must be going," she told Mrs. Hopkins. "When Ada wakes up, tell her I'll call again tomorrow."

★ ★ ★ ★ ★

"Bad news, Mrs. Lincoln," Henry Wilder commented, as the carriage made its way through the rainy streets, heading back toward the White House. "Young Mr. Belford's murder."

"Dreadful news," she told him. "Mrs. Belford is overwhelmed with grief. We must do what we can to find out who is responsible for the boy's death."

"You don't believe the murderer was an ordinary footpad?" Henry asked.

The First Lady shook her head. "It's far too convenient that Edward was found dead near Willard's Hotel."

Henry nodded. "I see. Mr. Grayson and his wife are staying at Willard's Hotel. I take it you wish me to find out whether Mr. Chester is staying there as well. And whether Major Markham has visited either of them recently."

"All three of them were together, as recently as this afternoon," Mrs. Lincoln said. "At the hospital, Edward told me he'd seen them together, in a tavern near the War Department. Edward saw his uncle handing money to Chester and the major. The three dots are already connected, and to no good end, I'm sure."

"It certainly points to more than a footpad in an alley off Fourteenth." The carriage halted at the White House. Henry stepped down, then helped her from the conveyance.

"Yes, but we must find out why, and how." Mrs. Lincoln bade him goodnight in the downstairs hallway. Mr. Lincoln, it seemed, was still tied up at the Capitol. The boys had eaten their dinner and gone to bed. Mrs. Lincoln asked for a light supper to be sent up to her room on a tray. As she climbed the stairs leading up to the family quarters, she wished she could discuss Edward Belford's murder with her husband, ask him for his advice and counsel. But she had no wish to add yet another burden to his load. He has so many other deaths on his mind.

It was still raining the next morning when the First Lady's seamstress arrived. Elizabeth Keckley was an ex-slave. Mrs. Lincoln, a southerner whose own family was divided on the issue of slavery, would not have thought it possible for two such dissimilar women to become friends. Yet they shared a closeness that Mrs. Lincoln had come to cherish.

Now Mrs. Lincoln needed Lizzie's services for something other than stitching seams. She told Lizzie about Edward's murder. "I can't go out unnoticed, of course. Not without Henry and those troopers. But you can. I've already sent Henry on an errand. But I must know where Edward went after he left the hospital yesterday afternoon. You must be my eyes and ears and feet, Lizzie."

Lizzie Keckley nodded, reaching for her shawl and reticule. That morning Mrs. Lincoln saw to her boys, then she had an appointment with Mr. William Wood, the acting commissioner of public buildings, who was assisting her with the refurbishment of the White House. In the afternoon she took tea with a group of congressmen's wives. By the time the women had left, the seamstress had returned from an information gathering mission. In fact, both Lizzie and Henry had information for her.

"I asked people who work in that hospital if they'd seen the young man," Lizzie said. "Couldn't get the time of day from those military people, so I went across the street. Found a grocer's boy who gave Mr. Belford directions to Willard's Hotel."

"So he was going there," Mrs. Lincoln said triumphantly. "To see his uncle, I'll be bound. What else?"

"The grocer's boy saw an enlisted man, a corporal, following Mr. Belford. This corporal was a big fellow with dark hair and a dark beard."

"Was the man was a hospital orderly?" Mrs. Lincoln asked. Hadn't she seen a man of that description, about the same time Edward met her at the hospital?

"I don't think so," Lizzie said. "The grocer's boy told me the man's uniform was too clean for him to be an orderly. The orderlies do get a bit worse for wear, working with the wounded."

Mrs. Lincoln turned to Henry Wilder. "Do you remember him, at the hospital?"

"I do," Henry said. "He was in the hallway the same time as Edward. I also assumed he was an orderly."

"This man followed Mr. Belford all the way to Willard's," Lizzie said. "You said the boy was killed near there, so I went to the hotel. A friend of mine works as a waiter, so I talked with him. Mr. Belford was there, all right, in the lobby. He looked like he was waiting for someone. Don't know if he ever met who he was waiting for, though. My friend didn't see him leave."

"John Grayson," Mrs. Lincoln said. "He went to see his uncle. Did your friend see the corporal who'd been following Edward?"

"Yes, he did. Noticed him, because he doesn't see many enlisted men in the lobby of Willard's. Says he followed the young man right in the door, then made himself scarce."

"Good work, Lizzie." Mrs. Lincoln turned to Henry Wilder. "We must find out who this corporal is," Mrs. Lincoln told Henry. "If I were to make a guess, I'd say he's on speaking terms with Major Markham. Direct your inquiries there."

"I will. As for what I found out this afternoon, Mr. Chester is indeed registered at Willard's Hotel. He has been seen in the bar with Mr. Grayson, on several occasions. But not with the major."

"Mr. Grayson's factory in Fall River makes woolen cloth," the First Lady said slowly. "Mr. Chester represents clothmakers. And I'll wager Major Markham's job is to procure cloth for Army uniforms."

"You would win that bet, Mrs. Lincoln," Henry said. "The major awards contracts to factories that make the uniforms. As for Mr. Chester, I was wrong to assume that he was an agent representing American woolen manufacturers. His clients are European. Now, I've heard talk during our hospital visits of a shortage of woolens for uniforms. Recently I've also heard there's a plan to purchase woolens from abroad."

"It's more than talk," Mrs. Lincoln told him. "And it's certain to make American woolen manufacturers angry. What if John Grayson found out about the government's plan to buy that cloth from the Europeans? What would he do to prevent that purchase?"

"Murder his own nephew?" Lizzie asked. No one answered her question.

"Go find out about that corporal," Mrs. Lincoln told Henry. "When you return, we'll decide what to do."

The rain had stopped falling later that evening when Mrs. Lincoln, accompanied by Henry Wilder and the Frontier Guard troopers, knocked on Olivia Hopkins' door. The Army officer's widow admitted her and told her that Ada Belford was asleep in the upstairs bedroom. "May I offer you some tea?"

"Thank you, yes," Mrs. Lincoln said, removing her gloves. "Make a large pot. There will be some people joining us."

Mrs. Hopkins narrowed her eyes and considered this, then she nodded, and left Mrs. Lincoln and Henry alone in the parlor, with the troopers standing guard in the vestibule. "I hope our scheme works," Mrs. Lincoln said.

"Lizzie and I delivered the messages," Henry told her. "Exactly as you instructed us. Were you able to speak with the President?"

Just as Mrs. Lincoln opened her mouth to answer, someone knocked at the door. One of the troopers made a move as though to answer, but Mrs. Lincoln forestalled him with a wave of her hand. Instead it was Mrs. Hopkins who hurried from her kitchen and opened the door to John Grayson.

"Why, John, I wasn't expecting you. Is Ella with you?"

"You sent me a note," the factory owner said, brows knitted in consternation. "You said it was urgent."

"It is, Mr. Grayson," Mrs. Lincoln said. "It was I who sent for you, not Mrs. Hopkins. Sit down. We're expecting other guests." She beckoned him to join her in the parlor. With a glance at the large trooper to his left, he reluctantly complied.

"I'll get the tea," Mrs. Hopkins said, frowning as she tried to piece together what was going on. She went back to the kitchen and returned quickly with the tea tray, which Henry took from her.

The door knocker sounded again. Mrs. Hopkins went to answer it. Major Charles Markham strode into the vestibule. He looked at the two troopers, startled, then into the parlor. His eyes widened slightly as he saw Grayson sitting there, with Mrs. Lincoln, Mrs. Hopkins and Henry Wilder. "What's going on? I got a message that Daisy was here and had been taken ill."

"I'm sorry for the subterfuge," Mrs. Lincoln said, "but it was necessary to get you here. Please join us, Major."

The officer scowled. "I have no time for this nonsense. I must get back to the War Department."

146

"You'd better sit down and hear me out," Mrs. Lincoln said, her voice cold. "It isn't nonsense. It's far more serious than that, and it concerns you and Mr. Grayson. And Mr. Chester, who won't be joining us. He's been detained."

When they heard this last name, the major's mouth tightened and Grayson's eyes became hooded. A look passed quickly between the two men. Mrs. Hopkins noticed. Her lips tightened as she looked at the First Lady. "Should I leave?" It was plain that she didn't want to.

Mrs. Lincoln shook her head. "No, I want you here, as a witness. To this plot to defraud the government. And murder Edward Belford."

Major Markham swore under his breath, causing the troopers near the door to move toward the parlor. At the same time Grayson rose to his feet, nearly upsetting the tea tray. "What are you talking about?"

Mrs. Lincoln cut both men off, her gesture as sharp as her words. "I overheard you and Mr. Chester at the White House reception, Mr. Grayson. You said there was a shortage of woolens and if the cards were played right, you'd all be rich. Then Mr. Chester said, 'Make it worth my while.' That's what you did, Mr. Grayson. And Edward saw you do it, in a tavern yesterday afternoon. You paid off Major Markham, no doubt for the information about the government's plan to purchase woolen cloth from abroad. As an American manufacturer, you'd prefer that transaction not take place. So you paid off Mr. Chester, the American agent who represents a consortium of European woolen merchants, to call off the deal."

The factory owner's dark face got white around the mouth.

Major Markham gave nothing away. "This is absurd," he said. "Nothing of the sort happened."

"You were seen, and you know it," Mrs. Lincoln said. 'Why else would you send Corporal Jackson to kill Edward Belford?"

"Kill Edward?" Grayson shouted. "Edward saw?"

"Yes, he did. And he told me, before he went to Willard's Hotel, to look for you. He was followed by Corporal Jackson. Who, as it happens, works in the procurement office at the War Department."

Grayson turned on Markham in horror. "You only told me we'd been seen. But you didn't say it was my nephew who'd observed us."

"Hold your tongue," the major snarled. "They have no proof for this story."

"All the proof *I* need is in your faces," Mrs. Hopkins said, revulsion in her eyes as she raked them over the major and her brother-in-law. "Your hands might as well be covered in blood."

"We do have proof," Mrs. Lincoln told them. "When I said Mr. Chester had been detained, I did not mean he was delayed. He's been arrested by the police, on the orders of the President himself. The authorities are on their way here now. Corporal Jackson has also been taken into custody, and I understand he's been quite vocal about it. You see, Major, your clerk has no intention of taking sole blame for this crime."

"Pack Rat" appeared in the e-anthology Compulsion. *Some years back I read an article about extreme hoarding disorder, which is a fancy term for being a pack rat. As anyone who has seen my office can attest, I know all about being a pack rat. The article was accompanied by a list of questions. If one answered yes to a certain number of those questions, one might have a problem, for which one might consider seeking help. I answered the questions. And no, I won't tell you how many yes answers there were in my tally.*

Pack Rat

When the neighbors saw rats climbing the curtains in the window of the house on Oak Street, they called the cops.

"I've complained and complained. Nobody does anything." Mrs. Halpern waved her hand at the offending sight. "Just look at that yard."

Officer Sylvia Wykoff put her hands on her hips and surveyed the house. It was a one-story wood-frame bungalow built in the 1930s or 1940s, a typical sight in this coastal city. The house had once been white, but now it was dingy gray, almost as dark as the blue trim surrounding the windows. Crab grass and weeds overwhelmed the yard. A dark green rosemary bush crouched to the left of the porch. On the right, an ivy vine wound around the porch support and extended its tendrils up the rainspout and along the gutters.

By contrast, Mrs. Halpern's yard was a testament to her skill as a gardener. The grass was green and manicured, no weeds in sight. Roses climbed a trellis near her porch, and a neatly trimmed bed of marigolds delineated the border between the two yards.

"That used to be a nice little house," Mrs. Halpern said to Sylvia and her partner, Officer Mike Madera. "The last tenants were a young couple with a baby. They kept the place up. But they moved. Had another baby on the way and the house just wasn't big enough."

Now she pointed an accusing finger at the piles of yellowed newspapers on the porch. "Then that man moved in.

151

The place has gone to hell in a handbasket, as my late husband would say. It's turned into a dump. I've called the owner several times, but he doesn't live here in town, and he's not interested in doing anything but collecting the rent. The yard is bad enough. But rats! That's absolutely the last straw. Somebody's got to do something."

"Yes, ma'am," Sylvia agreed patiently. The neighbors figured she and Mike were the somebodies who could do something. But as they both knew, there were procedures to follow in a situation such as this.

"See that car he's got parked in his driveway," Mr. Magruder chimed in. His house was to the right. "It doesn't run. He takes the bus. I've seen him at the bus stop on Water Street. This car turned up in the driveway a couple of months ago. He's been tinkering with it. He's got car innards everywhere, even on my property."

"Let's have a look," Mike said. He and Sylvia walked up the driveway, followed by Mr. Magruder. There was a detached garage, same vintage as the house, with the old-fashioned sort of side-by-side doors that opened outward. A plank fence sagged dispiritedly between the house and the garage. In the middle a half-open gate led to the back yard, as overgrown as the front.

They stopped at the rear of the rusting maroon vehicle. The back seat was completely covered with old newspapers, magazines and who knew what else.

"A Studebaker," Mike said. "Late forties. Cleaned up and restored it'd be a showpiece."

"Now it's a junker," Sylvia said.

The Studebaker certainly wasn't being used for transportation. It looked as thought it was simply used to store more junk, or cannibalized for whatever was under the hood. Car parts cluttered the driveway between the front of the vehicle and the garage. Some of them had encroached on the strip of weeds separating the driveway from Mr. Magruder's yard, which wasn't the showplace Mrs. Halpern's yard was. Where Mrs. Halpern had marigolds, Mr. Magruder had dandelions.

"I'm telling ya," Mr. Magruder was saying, "we just can't put up with this anymore. There oughta be a law."

"There is," Sylvia said. She wasn't sure just which laws might apply. If there were rats, as the neighbors claimed, that made it a health issue.

"Do you know the man's name?" Mike asked the neighbors as they walked back to the front yard. "What does he look like?"

Mrs. Halpern shook her head, and Mr. Magruder shrugged. "Don't know his name. He's a skinny guy with brown hair. Wears khaki slacks and a khaki jacket most of the time, and carries one of those backpacks. Brown, like his clothes."

Sylvia glanced at her watch. It was almost seven on a balmy spring evening. The guy should be home by now. Sylvia headed toward the porch, with Mike at her heels. The weeds waved lazily as they passed, and she caught the scent of rosemary as she brushed against the bush overhanging the sidewalk. Ivy tendrils loomed as though reaching out to draw her into a trap.

The two police officers stepped onto the porch, squeezing between the piles of newspapers. Sylvia touched the top of one pile. The newsprint felt as though it had been dampened by rain, then had dried to the consistency of papier-mâché. A couple of envelopes had fallen from the rusty metal mailbox next to the front door. She reached for them. "Occupant," read the first. No help there. However, the second one bore the name R. L. Sloan.

Sylvia passed the envelopes to Mike, who glanced at them,

153

then stuck them back into the mailbox. Then he pointed at the living room window. There, in the gap between the curtains, she saw a pair of beady black eyes. A rat.

She shuddered as the rat disappeared. This is a fine mess. Or an awful one, take your pick. Might as well get it over with. She rapped on the door. "Mr. Sloan? This is Officer Wykoff and Officer Madera. Open the door, please. We'd like to speak with you."

No response. She moved to the large front window, but all she could see now were several layers of dirt and grime streaking the glass.

"Break down the door, why doncha?" Mr. Magruder called.

Mrs. Halpern added her two cents. "Haul him and his junk off to the dump."

Sylvia decided now was not the most opportune time to give Mr. Sloan's neighbors a lecture about due process and probable cause. She knocked again. Then she tilted her head to one side and listened. She thought she'd heard a noise.

"Mr. Sloan, are you in there? Are you all right?"

There it was again, a thump. Someone—or something— was moving around inside.

"You hear that?"

Mike cocked his head. "Yeah."

She heard another thump, then the squeak of a floor board. There was a crash. Now came the unmistakable sound of footsteps pounding toward the back of the house.

Sylvia jumped off the porch and ran up the driveway, through the half-open gate. The back door opened. A figure dressed in completely in black, except for a bright orange ball cap that covered its head, streaked out the back door and sprinted through the waist-high foliage toward the low fence at the back of the lot.

"Hold it!" Sylvia plowed through the high weeds, Mike right behind her. Then her foot caught on something and she plunged forward, hands out as she tried to break her fall. A rake. Lucky the tines were down instead of up. She scrambled to her feet, saw the figure vault the fence into the alley, heading north. Mike followed. But when Sylvia reached the alley, he was walking back toward her, shaking his head.

"Took off like greased lightening. Gone by the time I got to the end of the block."

"Did you get a good look at him?" Sylvia asked.

"Could have been a her," Mike said. "Short and slender."

"That description fits a lot of men, too. All I saw was black clothes, and that orange ball cap."

"Orange? It looked red to me." Mike rubbed his chin thoughtfully. "Anyway, he—or she—was in good shape. Took that fence like it was a hurdle. Let's check the house and see what our visitor was up to."

The back door was ajar. Sylvia rapped on the doorjamb. "Mr. Sloan? Are you in there?"

What was that? Someone groaning? Or was she imagining things?

"Mr. Sloan?" Mike called. "It's Officer Madera and Officer Wykoff. Do you need assistance?"

Sylvia listened, but she didn't hear anything now. She pushed the door wider and stepped into a kitchen. At least, she thought it was a kitchen. She stopped to get her bearings, shaking her head in disbelief.

"How can anyone live like this?"

Mike located the light switch and illuminated the room. "I've seen worse. At least it doesn't stink."

Small mercies. Sylvia looked around her. The kitchen was about eight feet square, larger than the one in her apartment. But when it came to useable space, there wasn't any. Nearly every available surface—including the green linoleum floor, the counters, the kitchen table and the two chairs—was covered. A path about two feet wide had been left clear so that the occupant could move through the maze of this house.

"Why do people save this stuff?" she asked.

"Who knows?" Mike shrugged. "I knew a guy once, he saved soap slivers. Kept 'em in shoe boxes. Guess he was afraid of running out of soap. Now Mr. Sloan, he likes paper."

"Like it? He must be addicted to it." Sylvia shook her head.

Paper everywhere. Old magazines, old newspapers, books, both paperback and hardback. Pads of notepaper and discarded business forms. Calendars with dates five and ten years old. Cardboard boxes were stacked on the floor. The counters held coffee cans and an assortment of those plastic tubs that had once held food. Now they held rubber bands, and another held bits of string, while still others held coupons, old letters, paperclips, pencil stubs, tacks and pushpins. Under the kitchen table were several smaller boxes filled with paper of all sizes and colors. An assortment of stainless steel pots and pans covered the surface of the four-burner stove. Sylvia didn't even want to think about what was inside the cabinets.

"Watch out for the rats." Amusement colored Mike's voice.

Sylvia jumped. Mike grinned as he pointed toward one end of the counter, to the left of the sink. There she saw two rats, a white one with a pink nose, and a brown and white spotted one, huddled inside a metal cage, a big one, with wood chips at the bottom. The door was open and the rats hid in the corner behind their water dish and a raggedy stuffed bear. Next to the cage was a sack of kibble.

"Well, at least they're not the big ugly ones I've seen down by the waterfront," she said. "Or roof rats, like the ones that were living in the trees in City Park."

"They're pets. My kid brother, the one in high school, has a couple of rats. Only Mom won't let them roam the house, the way Sloan evidently lets his."

The rats chittered at them. Mike leaned over and shut the cage door. "No sense in letting them run loose, at least for the time being. Now all we have to do is find Sloan."

Now they heard sounds again—a thump, a groan, a quavering voice. "Help me. Please, help me."

They moved quickly into the living room. More stuff was piled everywhere, with a narrow path between, so that Sloan could navigate his cluttered, crowded environment. Several cardboard cartons next to an old rolltop desk had toppled. Underneath one of the boxes Sylvia saw a skinny man, with brown gabardine trousers, a brown knit shirt, and brown hair.

The hair was streaked with red—sticky bright red blood, oozing from a deep cut in the man's scalp, staining the dusty hardwood floor. Sylvia reached for her radio and called the paramedics and the crime scene techs.

Sylvia and Mike lifted the box off Sloan. The carton was heavy, full of books, it turned out. It could have been an accident, she thought. Easy enough to say the pack rat's stash had fallen on him. And then he'd hit his head on the corner of the desk on his way down. But she didn't see any blood on the desk. That black-clad figure running from the house must have had something do with Sloan's injury. Whoever it was had been raiding the pack rat's nest. But why?

"You think it was a robbery attempt?" Sylvia knelt and put her hand to Sloan's forehead, then felt for his pulse. Sloan's skin was clammy, his pulse fluttery. Though he was conscious, his brown eyes looked glazed. Concussion, she thought. She heard a siren in the distance, getting closer.

"Maybe." Mike glanced around him. "He's probably got stuff in there worth stealing. But who can tell? How are we going to find out if anything is missing?"

The man on the floor moaned again. Sylvia moved closer, peering into his eyes. "Mr. Sloan, can you tell me what happened?"

Sloan muttered something unintelligible. Then his eyes rolled up and the lids went down. "He's out," Mike said. "There's a wallet in his back pocket." He teased the leather folder from Sloan's pants and flipped it open, examining the contents. "Robert L. Sloan, according to his driver's license. Age forty-one. Health insurance card. Same plan as ours." Then he whistled. "Well, what do you know? Sloan works for the city, just like you and me. City engineer's office."

"Anything in there about relatives?" Sylvia asked. "As in who to call in an emergency?"

Mike shook his head. "Nope. No pictures, no emergency card. Here's a business card, though. Laura Fitch, Behavior Therapy. An office on Walnut Street. Her home number's written on back."

Sylvia tucked the card into her pocket. "We'll call her when we get to the hospital." The siren got louder, then stopped in front of the house. Mike opened the front door as the paramedics trotted up the front sidewalk.

"Holy jumping Jehosephat!" The first EMT stared into the living room. "How the hell are we supposed to get him out?"

"I don't know," Mike snapped. "Just get in here and treat the man. He's got a bad cut on the head, and probably a concussion. Then you can be creative and figure out how to get him out to your rig."

In the end the paramedics wound up putting Sloan on a stretcher and lifting him high over his clutter, through the front door, to the ambulance waiting outside. The crime scene techs had arrived by then. "You have got to be kidding," one of them muttered when he saw the house.

"No, I'm not," Sylvia told him. "Pay attention to the back door. The intruder went out that way."

The techs grumbled as they set to work, dusting for prints. They collected what evidence they could. Sylvia found a set of keys hanging on the doorknob in Sloan's bedroom. One of the keys fit the front door.

"Wonder if he had any keys on him," Mike said.

"If he did, the intruder took them," Sylvia guessed.

The two officers moved through the house one last time, making sure the doors and windows were locked before they left.

"What are we going to do about the rats?" Sylvia asked when they were in the kitchen. The creatures, rattled by all the strangers in the house, hunkered down in the wood chips at the bottom of the cage.

Mike grinned. "You want to take them home?"

"My cats would go ballistic. It's just that I wouldn't want anything to happen to them. Since they're his pets."

"They'll be okay. We'll check on them first thing in the morning."

They made sure the rats had plenty of water, and filled one of the plastic containers with kibble from the sack. Then they headed for Community Hospital.

"It's a concussion, all right," the emergency room doctor told them. "The wound in his scalp took twelve stitches. He hasn't regained consciousness yet. Does he have family?"

"We don't know." Sylvia pulled the business card they'd found from her pocket. "Maybe this therapist can tell us."

She found a phone and punched in the number that was written on the back of the card. She got an answering machine. Sylvia identified herself and started to leave a message about Sloan being injured. Then there was a click. A woman's voice said, "This is Laura Fitch. You're at the hospital? I'll be there in fifteen minutes."

When she arrived, Laura Fitch turned out to be a woman of about forty, with short salt-and-pepper hair and an air of confidence. She was dressed for an evening out, in blue silk pants with a matching blouse. Her high heels clicked as she crossed the floor to where the two officers stood, outside Sloan's room.

"Thank you so much for calling to tell me about Robert," she said. "I was concerned that something like this would happen."

"Why?" Mike asked.

"People with Robert's condition sometimes hurt themselves."

It was likely that someone else had hurt Sloan, but Sylvia kept that thought to herself for the time being, letting Ms. Fitch assume that Sloan's injuries were due to an accident. "What sort of condition are you talking about?"

"As you may have guessed from the state of his home," Laura Fitch said, "Robert suffers from extreme hoarding disorder."

"You mean he's a pack rat," Mike said.

"I'm afraid it's more serious than that." The corners of the therapist's mouth drew down, as though to emphasize the gravity of Sloan's condition.

Mike nodded. "Yeah. It sure looked serious. You say it's a disorder?"

"Absolutely," Fitch told them. "In fact, it's so prevalent, I specialize in treating it. When clutter becomes more than ordinary, it's extreme hoarding—and it's definitely a problem. As police officers, surely you've seen situations where some poor soul is living a house that is so filthy and cluttered that the authorities are called in."

Sylvia nodded. "That's why we went to Mr. Sloan's house. The neighbors saw his pet rats at the window, and thought they were the other kind of rats. Why does Mr. Sloan save that stuff?"

"It's hard to say." Fitch's voice took on a professorial tone. "Like many people with this disorder, Robert considers himself a saver, a thrifty person. He saves things that have no value to someone like me. But he values them. He has anxiety attacks at the thought of throwing anything away. He's an engineer. Among men, engineers seem to be susceptible. Among women, I've seen librarians, teachers, artists. I'm not at liberty to discuss Robert's case in detail, but in general terms, I can tell you that extreme hoarding can stem from a number of sources, such as obsessive-compulsive disorder, depression, dementia or a drug or alcohol problem."

"How do you treat something like that?" Mike asked.

"Behavior therapy," Fitch said. "In some cases medication. In fact, with some of my clients, I often find it useful to go to their houses and help them clean. But it isn't easy to get people into treatment. Most hoarders don't even recognize they have a problem. Fortunately Robert is beginning to understand that his saving things is interfering with his life. It has certainly alienated him from his family. He came to me for help, about a month ago. I haven't been working with him very long. But I think we're making some progress."

Sylvia recalled the condition of Sloan's house. If Fitch had been helping Sloan clean the place, they hadn't made as much progress as the therapist seemed to think.

"We'd like to contact his family," Mike said. "Do you

have a name, a number?"

"His parents are no longer living, but there's a sister in another state. I don't have a name or number. Perhaps his office . . . But surely Robert could tell you that himself."

"I'm afraid he's still unconscious," Mike said. "We'll be asking him some questions as soon as he wakes up."

"Do you have any information on this hoarding thing?" Sylvia asked. "Just so we can put it in our report."

"Certainly." Fitch reached into her shoulder bag, and fished out a folded page that turned out to be a photocopy of a story from the local newspaper. "I was interviewed on this subject last year, and I carry a few copies with me."

"Pays to advertise, right?" Mike said with a grin.

Fitch responded with a flinty smile and handed the article to Sylvia. "I think you'll find this very informative. Now, if you'll excuse me, it's rather late."

After she'd gone, Sylvia glanced at the article and the accompanying photograph of Laura Fitch. To the right of the photograph she saw a sidebar, with a headline that read, "The warning signs of extreme hoarding." The legend underneath told her that if she answered yes to two or more of the questions below, she might have a hoarding problem, and should consider seeking help. She glanced through the eleven warning signs listed and tallied up her yes answers.

"Damn. Guess what I'm doing on my next day off?"

Mike chuckled. "Cleaning your apartment?"

"You got it."

"And how many of those questions were a yes?"

"None of your business."

"What's your take on Fitch?" Mike asked the next morning as they drove over to Sloan's house. "Is she legit? I mean, I never heard of a therapist who specializes in pack rats. I wouldn't think she'd get that much business."

"According to her, she does." Sylvia stopped for a red light. "It looks like she's on the up-and-up. I checked her out with the state licensing board. I talked with the landlord at her office building on Walnut. And I did a search on the Internet. She's written several long articles on the subject. You know, the kind in scholarly journals, lots of dense prose. Seems like Fitch and her ex-husband are the experts on the subject in this part of the country."

"Ex-husband, huh? When did they split up? And why?"

"The landlord says last year. Over another woman. His, not hers. Nasty divorce, the landlord says. A lot of squabbling over who got to keep which clients. According to the landlord, our Ms. Fitch came out with the short end of the stick. Client-wise and money-wise. She had to move into a smaller office."

Sylvia parked the cruiser in front of Sloan's house and they went inside to check on the rats. The creatures seemed glad to see the humans. As Sylvia and Mike locked the front door, Mr. Magruder walked over from his house. "Somebody tried to get in there last night," he told them. "Around midnight. Heard a noise, looked out my bedroom window, saw some fella in black walking up the driveway. Slipped into the back yard. I went out and hollered at him. He took off down the alley."

"You sure it was a man?" Mike traded looks with Sylvia.

"Not positive," Mr. Magruder said. "Had a ball cap on his head, though."

"Orange?" Sylvia asked. "Or red?"

Mr. Magruder shook his head. "Too dark to tell."

They checked the house but didn't see any signs of attempts at forced entry. "Which we wouldn't if whoever attacked Sloan took his keys," Mike said. "Looks like our intruder didn't get what he was after."

"Nope," Sylvia said. "Question is, what was he after?"

At the hospital, Sloan's doctor told them his patient was still unconscious. "I'm concerned about a subdural hematoma. And he didn't hit his head on the desk. He was struck with a blunt object."

"I figured as much," Mike said. "The techs didn't find any blood on that desk. As for blunt objects, the house was full of 'em."

"Could have been anything," Sylvia said. "If the intruder tossed it across the room it could take us months to find it. I wish he'd wake up, so he could tell us what happened."

"I'll call you as soon as he does," the doctor assured them.

Sloan's supervisor in the city engineer's office was a man named Arles. "I was beginning to wonder," he told the two officers when they showed up at the sprawling modern city office complex downtown. "Robert's punctual. He'd call if he wasn't coming in. How is he?"

They told him Sloan had a concussion and asked about information on Sloan's next of kin. "Sure. I'll take you to the personnel office." He led the way down a corridor. "That's Robert's office right there," Arles said.

Then he frowned and stopped suddenly. From the expression on his face, Sylvia guessed that Arles had expected Sloan's door to be locked and the office dark. Instead the door was ajar and the light was on. A woman in a green dress was seated at Sloan's desk, muttering to herself as she rooted around through the papers on the desk's surface. She evidently hadn't found whatever she was looking for. That was because Sloan's office looked a lot like Sloan's house.

The supervisor pushed the door wider, glancing down at the knob, as though wondering how she'd gotten in. "This is

Coral Baldwin," he added, turning toward the officers. "She works with Robert. Are you looking for something, Coral?"

"That report on the Patterson job," she snapped. "He was supposed to give it to me day before yesterday. Which he didn't. So where the hell is he, and that damned report?"

"Robert's out sick," the supervisor said, choosing his words carefully. "We don't know when he'll be back in the office."

Coral Baldwin pushed the chair away from the desk and stood. Her eyes moved from Arles to the two police officers, assessing them. "So Robert had an accident, huh? What did he do, trip over something? If his house is as big a mess as this office, I'm not surprised."

The woman had been quick to guess that Sloan was out due to an accident, Sylvia thought, even though Arles told her Sloan was sick. Maybe it was more than guessing. Sloan's coworker was short and her legs were muscular above a pair of sensible flat heels. A runner, perhaps? She had dark hair that could easily be tucked out of sight under a ball cap. Was she really after a report in Sloan's desk, or looking for something else?

Sylvia glanced at Mike and knew he was thinking the same thing. "Well, accidents happen," Mike said easily. "We just stopped by to get the name and number of Mr. Sloan's next of kin. Not that it's that serious. But he'll be in the hospital a couple of days."

"Personnel, right," Arles said, back on course and motioning them to follow. "They'll be able to give you that information."

Sloan in the hospital for a couple of days meant the house would be unoccupied for a couple of nights. Unless you counted the rats. Sylvia and Mike were hoping the intruder didn't. "What makes you so sure the perp will be back for

165

another try?" their sergeant asked that afternoon.

"He's looking for something he hasn't found yet," Mike said. "I'll be outside, Officer Wykoff will be inside."

There was an alcove in the hallway of Sloan's house. Sylvia squeezed in between a coat rack and an old chest of drawers, and adjusted her position until she had a clear view of the kitchen and part of the living room. Mike was outside, watching the house. An hour ticked by. The only sounds Sylvia heard were Sloan's rats, chittering in their cage in the kitchen.

Then came another noise from the kitchen, a key snicking in the lock, the back door opening. A flashlight played against the wall. Sylvia held her breath. So she and Mike were right. Whoever had attacked Sloan had taken his keys and the set they found in the bedroom was a duplicate. As she peered at the figure moving in the kitchen she halfway expected to see Sloan's coworker, Coral Baldwin, who'd evidently gotten past the locked door of Sloan's office at work. But the figure in black sweats, hair covered by a black ball cap, was Laura Fitch.

Sylvia recalled last night at the hospital, when the therapist was telling the officers about treatment for extreme hoarding disorder. "With some of my clients," she'd said, "I often find it useful to go to their houses and help them clean."

Useful, indeed. Fitch was doing more than helping Sloan clean. Housework wasn't on her agenda tonight.

Fitch made her way carefully through the maze. In the living room, she stopped at the desk, shining the flashlight beam on its cluttered surface. Then she shrugged out of the backpack she was wearing. She fingered Sloan's keys, trying one after another in the first of the four drawers that ranged down the lower left side of the desk. Pulling open the drawer, she rummaged inside, removing an envelope. She shoved the envelope into the backpack and shut the drawer. She repeated the procedure with the rest of the drawers. Then she put the pack on her back and turned to leave the way she'd come.

"Police! Stop right there." Sylvia stepped from her hiding place, blocking the way to the back door. Fitch grabbed a book and threw it at Sylvia. Then she made a dash for the front door and flung it open. But the clutter on the front porch slowed her down. Mike tackled her on the overgrown lawn.

"What's she got in that pack?" Mike asked as he cuffed Fitch.

Sylvia unzipped the black nylon and took a look. "Bonds, stock certificates, some bank books." She whistled. "Our Mr. Sloan is worth quite a bit."

"Of course he is," Mike said. "Our Mr. Sloan is a saver." He hauled Fitch to her feet. "You're a big help, Ms. Therapist. Looks like you were helping yourself."

Short as she was, Fitch managed to look down her nose at him. She compressed her lips and said nothing, until they got her down to headquarters and she demanded her lawyer.

They spent most of the next day putting together the pieces, starting with Fitch's ex-husband, who taught psychology at the college in the next town. He required some persuading, but finally he told them he suspected his former wife of using her therapy sessions to find out which clients had valuables so she could steal them later, when she visited their overcrowded homes. In fact one client had mentioned, long after the fact, that she was missing some jewelry, and she suspected Fitch. "But she never reported it to the police. I think she was afraid of her hoarding disorder becoming common knowledge."

167

"Aren't you supposed to report things like that?" Mike asked.

Fitch's ex reluctantly admitted that he should have. "I thought was an isolated incident. And I had no proof."

The incidents weren't isolated, they discovered. Laura Fitch's finances were in bad shape. To augment her income, she'd been stealing valuables from half a dozen clients, pack rats like Sloan, who didn't even know the items were missing until they got a visit from the police, and took inventory.

"What a scam," Sylvia said at the end of the day. "Hurting people who are trying to help themselves."

That evening the doctor called to tell them Sloan was awake and out of danger. Sylvia and Mike went over to the hospital to tell him what had happened. But the thin brown man lying in the hospital bed seemed to be more concerned about his rats than the valuables that had almost been stolen from him.

"They're good company. The rest of it is just paper. That's what I tell myself when I try to throw things away." An anxious look flickered in Sloan's eyes, as though the thought of getting rid of anything pained him. "I know I'm a pack rat. It drives people crazy. Sometimes it makes me crazy, too. So I thought I'd do something about it. I did some research, then I saw that article in the paper. I answered yes to almost all those warning sign questions. And when I read about her treating people like me, she sounded like the person who could help me."

Sylvia glanced at Mike. They'd heard the same story over and over from Fitch's victims.

"We had several sessions in her office," Sloan went on. "Then she said we needed to confront my clutter in person. She came to my house. She was looking at my desk, admiring it because it's old. She tried the drawers and asked why they were locked. So I told her that's where I kept my important things, like the stock certificates. The second time she came over, the other night, she wanted me to open the drawer. When I said I didn't see any reason to open it, she hit me in the head with a bookend and took my keys from my pocket. She was trying to open the desk drawers when you two knocked on the door." Sloan sighed. "I should have been more careful."

"I'm sorry she didn't turn out to be the person who could help you," Sylvia said. "But there are other people who can. I called the local mental health association. Here's a list of therapists they recommend."

Sloan hesitated, then he took the list and thanked her. "I do want help."

"You've already taken the first step," she said, "and that's a big one."

"Think he'll call one of those therapists?" Mike asked as they left the hospital.

"I hope so," Sylvia said. "I'm sure of one thing, though."

"What's that?"

She laughed. "He'll never throw that list away."

"By the Book" appeared in the anthology Sisters in Crime IV *and* The Best of Sisters in Crime. *I spent eight years in the Navy, four as a petty officer in the journalist rating, and four as an officer. After Officer Candidate School in Newport, Rhode Island I attended Legal Officer School, and learned, among other things, how to conduct an investigation. I never thought I'd use that training, but while I was stationed at Treasure Island, near San Francisco, I did. My investigation didn't turn out the way the one in the story does, but I've worked for many a Dragon Lady. Who hasn't?*

By the Book

"It would make a lot of people happy if Slater didn't commit suicide," Dinah Gray said.

"Did she?" Meg asked.

"I don't know." Dinah toyed with her fork. "That's what my investigation is supposed to determine, if I remember what we were taught at Naval Justice School."

The two women, Navy lieutenants, had been roommates at Officer Candidate School, attending the short legal officer course afterwards. OCS friendships often disappeared after training, but Dinah and Meg kept in touch. Now they were both stationed at Bay Area Navy commands—Meg at Naval Air Station Alameda and Dinah at Treasure Island, the Navy base in the middle of San Francisco Bay. This Monday evening they sat at Dinah's kitchen table, sharing spaghetti and a bottle of wine. A third place had been laid for Dinah's husband Rob, an attorney, but he was working late.

"It's not as though I'm a legal pro." Dinah ran her fingers through her short blond hair as Meg refilled the wine glasses. "Command legal officer is a collateral duty, like public affairs officer. You know how it is at a small command. Anything major goes to the Navy lawyers, the ones who passed the bar exam. That's what I get for being the junior lieutenant."

"Other duties as assigned . . ." Meg smiled and quoted the phrase inherent to the job description of any Navy unrestricted line officer. It meant that junior officers could be assigned any number of unspecified tasks.

"I never thought I'd have to investigate someone's death."
Dinah shook her head. "I wish Slater hadn't driven her car
into San Francisco Bay."

But she had, last Friday, at approximately four o'clock on
a cold, clear February afternoon. According to the sole eyewitness, a sailor out for a jog around Treasure Island, Petty
Officer Ginny Slater floored the accelerator on her red Chevrolet Camaro, sped through a stop sign and up the sloping
breakwater on the island's perimeter. Slater and her car
soared toward the cold, choppy bay. The car landed nose
first, some thirty yards offshore, where it quickly sank. Navy
and Coast Guard search and rescue teams, summoned by the
witness, located the vehicle, its position shifted by the strong
currents that swept through the Golden Gate, out to sea.
When they hoisted the Camaro out of the water Slater's body
was still in the driver's seat, strapped in place by shoulder and
lap belt, wearing high-heeled pumps and a service dress blue
uniform.

Meg shuddered. "I can think of better ways to commit suicide."

"If she committed suicide. It could have been an accident.
What a way to die." Both women were quiet for a moment,
imagining death by drowning. Dinah had seen photographs
of the body, a sight that would stay with her for the rest of her
life. She reached for her wine. "I wonder why she was in dress
blues. The enlisted personnel in her department wear
working uniforms."

Various investigations were in progress, involving the base
police and the Naval Investigative Service. Dinah's command had to conduct its own investigation as well, standard
practice when one of the command's personnel died of something other than natural causes. The procedure was outlined
in the military Judge Advocate General Manual, and the

resulting report was submitted up the chain of command to Washington. The Dragon Lady had dumped the job on Dinah this morning.

The Dragon Lady was a tall slender woman edging toward fifty, if she hadn't reached it already. Her hair was an artful amalgam of brown and silver, coifed over a face that didn't leave her quarters without its full complement of makeup. She looked steely and capable in her impeccably-tailored uniforms, impressive with the four gold stripes of a captain around the cuffs. Having obtained that rank, the Dragon Lady was determined to join the rarified company of the few women to make admiral in what was still referred to as "this man's Navy."

Dinah had dubbed the captain the Dragon Lady shortly after reporting aboard the command last year. She was certain the older woman would walk over her own grandmother in high-heeled pumps in order to make admiral. "And if she does," Dinah once told Meg, "we'll have to kiss the hem of her dress blues."

Dinah cleared the table and made a pot of coffee. She and Meg moved to the living room, and the conversation shifted to other subjects. Meg left just as Rob came up the front steps. Dinah greeted him with a kiss, then husband and wife talked about their respective days while Rob ate his reheated dinner. Later, as Dinah loaded the dishwasher, her thoughts swirled around her unwelcome assignment. She'd never conducted a JAG Manual investigation before. The hypothetical exercises students did at the legal officer course didn't really count. It shouldn't be that difficult, though. The procedures were outlined in the manual.

I'll just go by the book, Dinah told herself. I'll talk to the witness, and Slater's supervisors and co-workers. I'll go over the reports and statements. It's just a matter of sifting through what's there. Routine. But she knew it wasn't going to be routine. The pressure was already on.

That afternoon the executive officer, Commander Fox, had called her into his office and made it plain the command would prefer an investigation that concluded Slater's death was accidental. After all, why would the young woman kill herself? She was a good worker, a first-class petty officer with ten years in the Navy, a "4.0 sailor" who routinely received the highest ratings on her performance evaluations. Nothing in her behavior over the past few weeks indicated anything was amiss. Besides, it was obvious the accelerator of the car stuck. Perhaps the seatbelt release had jammed, or Slater had hit her head when the car went into the water. Underneath Commander Fox's words was the unspoken message that there must be some reason Ginny Slater hadn't tried to save herself.

"The car is being checked over thoroughly, Commander," Dinah told him. "That should determine whether there were any mechanical problems."

What do you expect me to do? she thought. I can't believe Slater killed herself either. But I'm not going to lie or cover something up, just to suit you and the captain.

Tuesday morning Dinah sat at her desk with a mug of coffee and read through Ginny Slater's service record. Slater was twenty-eight, single, and lived in the Bachelor Enlisted Quarters on base. She had been at the command six months. Her previous assignment was a ship, a submarine tender, homeported in Guam. Tenders didn't go to sea as often as other ships and women at sea were restricted to non-combatants. So the Treasure Island billet was shore duty, something a lot of sailors coveted. There was no evidence that Slater had ever had any disciplinary problems. After boot camp she had attended various training schools and she had consistently advanced to the next higher rating each time she took the necessary exams.

Not much to go on, Dinah thought, as she drank the last cold mouthful of coffee. Nothing here that would indicate Slater took her own life. No note, either at work or in Slater's quarters. But whoever said suicide was logical?

Later that day Dinah talked to the eyewitness. He was barely eighteen, a lanky seaman apprentice with a faceful of freckles and a scrubbed fresh look, as though he was just off a Midwestern farm. The older Dinah got, the younger the sailors looked. "Tell me what you saw."

The sailor, who had already told his story many times to many people, took a deep breath and prepared to tell it again. "I was jogging near that intersection when I heard an engine rev up. I saw this red Camaro coming toward me, moving fast. I could only see one person in it, the driver. She zoomed right through that stop sign at the end of the road and flew up over the breakwater." The sailor's hand traced an arc in the air. "The car went into the water, nose first. I ran for the nearest phone, to call for help."

Dinah consulted the base police report, though by now she knew it by heart. "Can you describe the driver?"

"Yeah. I got a good look at her as she whizzed past. A good-looking brunette in dress blues. She had the shoulder harness fastened."

"Did the car sound all right?"

"Sounded like a car," the sailor said, with a shrug. "I mean, it didn't sound like there was anything wrong with it. She just revved it up real fast."

"You told the base police that the car began to sink almost immediately. Was it so fast that the driver didn't have a chance to get out?"

"She would have had time." The sailor frowned as he tried to recall every detail of the incident. "If she'd gotten the seatbelt unfastened she could have come out the driver's side window. It was down all the way."

"Are you sure?" Dinah looked at the report again. This bit of information was missing from the sailor's previous statement to the base police. And the description of the Camaro's condition after being pulled out of the bay indicated the driver's side window was at midpoint, as though Slater had attempted to lower it in an effort to get out of the car.

"Yeah, I'm sure," the sailor said, after thinking about it for a moment. He moved his arms and hands, grasping an imaginary steering wheel to show Dinah what he meant. "She had her right hand on the wheel of the car, like this, and her left arm resting on the window, you know, with the elbow sticking out."

Slater's division officer was a senior lieutenant named Turlock, round-faced and round-shouldered. He looked at Dinah over the disarray of his desk, with an impatient stare she translated to mean that he didn't have time for this and didn't want to discuss it anyway.

"You know why I'm here," she said.

He nodded. "Slater's car accident."

"What can you tell me about her?"

"A good worker. Never had any problems with her." Turlock rattled off the words as though he'd been preparing the statement.

"What sort of a person was she?"

"Hell, I don't know. She hadn't been here that long. I only saw her in a work situation. She got the job done and she got along with everyone."

"What about Slater's mood during the past several weeks?

Was there any indication that something might be bothering her?"

Turlock frowned. "I didn't notice anything. Why all these questions? It was an accident, right?"

"She didn't approach you about a problem?"

"For crying out loud, Lieutenant, if Slater had a problem she would talk to Chief Belsen, not me. That's why we have a chain of command. The chief sifts through the day-to-day stuff and doesn't bother me with anything that's not important."

I wouldn't come to you with a problem either, Dinah thought as she left Turlock's office. The lieutenant had evidently filed Slater's death under the heading of "day-to-day stuff," so she sought out his department's chief petty officer. She found Belsen at the coffee urn in the lounge, in conversation with several other chiefs. As she paused in the open doorway the conversation stopped. She felt like an interloper, a woman intruding on a men's gathering, an officer in an enlisted area.

"Chief Belsen, I'd like to talk with you."

"Yes, ma'am." Belsen set his mug down and joined her in the corridor. He was a wiry man with thinning hair, the left breast pocket of his khaki uniform heavy with ribbons and awards.

"Let's go to my office," Dinah said. She felt more comfortable on her own turf. Once there, she sat down at her desk and Belsen took the chair opposite. "I'm doing the JAG Manual investigation on Slater. You were her leading chief. What can you tell me about her?"

Belsen echoed Lieutenant Turlock's comments about Slater being a good worker. That's all Dinah had heard since beginning her investigation, and the phrase was beginning to make her impatient. The fact that Slater did her job didn't tell

Dinah much about the woman who drove her car into the
bay.

"What about Slater's mood, her behavior during the past
few weeks? Was something bothering her?"

"Well, who knows with women?" Belsen stopped and
looked embarrassed. His words didn't surprise Dinah. The
chief was the kind of old salt who had trouble adjusting to
women in the Navy, let alone women in his particular spe-
cialty, which had traditionally been male. "Beg your pardon,
ma'am, I just mean she was a little moody every now and
then. Her work had gotten a bit slipshod, like she didn't have
her mind on things. Not much, but enough so's I took her
aside and told her she better bring it up to snuff. Told her I
didn't want to have to lower her performance evals."

"Why was Slater's work slipping?"

"I don't know, Lieutenant. I only know that it was and I
told her to shape up."

"You weren't interested in finding out why?"

"Lieutenant," Belsen said, "I make it a point not to let my
personal problems interfere with the job. I tell my people the
same thing and I treat 'em all alike, men and women. The
Navy comes first. If something was wrong outside the job it
was up to Slater to take care of it."

Dinah tapped her pencil against the lined pad. In her years
in the Navy she had heard the same sentiments expressed
over and over again, in many ways. The Navy came first. She
understood the need to focus on the job. It was like that in
the civilian world too, if her husband's devotion to his law
firm was any indication. But in the real world people had
problems that cracked the surface of routine and job. Sometimes people fell through those cracks. Maybe Slater was
one of them. She was about to tell Belsen she had no more
questions when she remembered the question she had

expressed to Meg over dinner.

"Why was Slater wearing a dress uniform that day? Don't your people usually wear working uniforms?"

Belsen looked uncomfortable. "Well, she wanted to see the CO," he said, using the Navy shorthand for commanding officer.

"Why? Did she see the captain?"

"No, to both questions. She wouldn't say why. I told her she had to go by the book, put in a request chit to see the captain, and have me and Lieutenant Turlock approve it. The CO wasn't going to talk to Slater unless whatever it was couldn't be resolved by me, the lieutenant or the executive officer. That's why we have a chain of command, to solve these things at the lower levels. Now, how was I gonna resolve something when Slater wouldn't tell me what it was?"

"What other requests had Slater made during the past few months?"

"She wanted two weeks' leave, couple of months ago. Had to turn her down. I couldn't spare her right then, certainly not for two weeks."

"Anything else?"

Belsen hesitated. He looked away from her, mouth pursed like he'd tasted something sour. "She kept talking about a transfer. Never actually requested one, but there was no way she would have gotten it. She'd been here less than a year, and she was needed in this billet. Couldn't understand it. This is shore duty and she'd just come off a ship. Most sailors would love a billet like this. But Slater wanted orders somewhere in Florida. I certainly wouldn't have approved it. And I can't see the lieutenant or the captain going for it."

Dinah doubted it too. She understood the reason for Belsen's attitude, though she didn't entirely agree with it. The Navy didn't like people who requested transfers right after arriving at a duty station. You were supposed to complete your tour and not ask for special favors, because the organization ran on its own rhythm and routine. If you made waves you might swamp the boat. Dinah sometimes thought the organization needed to be more accommodating, but the Navy had been steaming along on tradition for over two hundred years. It didn't change easily.

The Dragon Lady and Commander Fox shared a suite of offices in the back corner of the building and the services of a civilian secretary named Lorraine. Wednesday Dinah asked Lorraine if she could speak with the Dragon Lady.

"I need to ask her some questions about her statement to the base police," Dinah said. "It's for my JAG Manual investigation." Given Chief Belsen's information about Slater's desire to see the captain, she wanted to confirm whether the Dragon Lady had in fact talked with her. The captain's statement indicated that she had seen Slater in the corridor outside Lieutenant Turlock's office early that morning and again just before lunch, but she didn't say anything about that afternoon. It wouldn't hurt to double check.

"She's gone to a meeting," Lorraine said. "I'll call you when she gets back."

"Did you see Petty Officer Slater that afternoon?" Dinah asked.

Lorraine shook her head. "No. But I left early, at two-thirty. I had a doctor's appointment. Maybe the exec saw her."

Dinah paused at the open door to Commander Fox's office. She knocked, then entered at a signal from the executive officer. She posed her question, but Fox told her he'd been out of the office that afternoon, and he couldn't recall seeing Ginny Slater earlier in the day. Fox asked how the investigation was progressing and told her the captain would like to have it finished by Monday.

"That shouldn't be a problem," she assured him.

Dinah interviewed various members of the command's enlisted staff Wednesday and Thursday. Most of them claimed they didn't know Slater well. That wasn't surprising, given the dead woman's short tenure. But she sensed that some of those she approached were reluctant to talk with her. Finally one man, a first-class petty officer named Bryce who was new to the command, told her if she wanted to talk, he'd buy her a cup of coffee.

She met him Thursday after work at a coffee shop in Oakland. Dusk settled over the city and a fine misty rain beaded on her uniform cap and the gold lieutenant's bars on the shoulders of her coat. Bryce had changed from his working uniform into blue jeans and an Oakland A's sweatshirt. He sat alone at a table near the window. Dinah shook the moisture from her cap and set it on the floor next to her purse. The waitress brought cups and filled them with coffee.

"Thanks for meeting me, Petty Officer Bryce."

"Hey, we're off duty." He grinned. "Call me Nick."

"Okay, Nick." She didn't tell him to call her Dinah. They were probably the same age and education level but she was still an officer, caught up in the tradition that separated the commissioned from the enlisted ranks, forbidding things like fraternization and familiarity. "What can you tell me about Ginny Slater?"

"We were friends," he said, lightening his coffee with cream. "We went out a few times, movies, dinner, a drink after work. I would have liked a different kind of relationship, but Ginny had other things on her mind."

"Such as?" Dinah burned her tongue on the coffee.

"A man," Bryce said, his tone implying that there was

always a man. "Ginny was involved with someone she met on Guam. I think his name was Jeff and I think he was an officer. She never did make that clear. Officers aren't supposed to fraternize with enlisted women. Or men." Bryce stopped and sipped his coffee, his eyes amused over the cup as he regarded Dinah.

"Anyway, from what little I do know, it sounded like they had some history. Ginny wanted to continue the relationship, but it's hard to do that long-distance. After Guam this guy Jeff transferred to Naval Air Station Jacksonville. Ginny tried to get leave a couple of months ago, to go back to Florida and see him. But she couldn't get away."

"I heard she wanted a transfer to Jacksonville."

Bryce nodded. "Or somewhere in Florida. She thought if she could just be in the same general location, the relationship would go back to the way it was. But I had a feeling it was over. It wouldn't surprise me if this guy was married."

"What makes you think that?"

"She didn't talk about it much and I'm making some guesses on my own," Bryce admitted. "But a person in love is not supposed to be as miserable as Ginny Slater was. She was unhappy, and it got worse over the past few months. There were days at work when she was so depressed she could barely function. I told her once if she ever wanted to unload, I have a great shoulder for crying on. She never took me up on it." Bryce shook his head. "What can you do? It was her business. I didn't want to stick my nose in—or my two cents' worth. Then, last week, Ginny got a letter from this guy. It sent her into a tailspin."

"What was in it?" Dinah asked, leaning forward.

"I don't know. To tell you the truth, I looked for that letter after Ginny drove her car into the drink. I went through her desk. Not thoroughly, because I was doing it on the sly before the guys in her department cleaned out all her personal stuff. But I couldn't find it. I talked to a friend of mine who's with the base police. He says they didn't find any letters from this guy Jeff in her room in the enlisted quarters. But who knows how carefully they looked, or what Ginny did with her mail. Maybe she pitched it. I don't know what Jeff wrote, but whatever it was, it sent her over the edge." Bryce narrowed his eyes. "You going to say Ginny killed herself? Or that it was an accident?"

"You think she committed suicide?"

"Hell, yes. She floored it and drove the damn car into the bay. What else could it be?"

"Maybe the accelerator stuck. Maybe she couldn't get the seat belt unfastened." Dinah tossed the sentences on the table merely for argument's sake, though she no longer believed these possibilities. That afternoon she had visited the on-base garage where Slater's car had been towed. The mechanic said he'd found nothing wrong with the engine or the seat belt that could conveniently be blamed for the incident. She also had a copy of the preliminary autopsy report. The shoulder harness had prevented Slater's head from striking the windshield, thus making it unlikely that the dead woman had been knocked unconscious. She could have released the belt and escaped through the window.

What about that window? Dinah wondered. All the way down as Slater drove her car into the bay, and half-open when the car, her body strapped in the driver's seat, was winched out of the water. Was Slater trying to get out of the car? Or keep herself in?

Bryce's words brought her back to the present. "That's why a lot of the enlisted guys won't talk to you. They think the command's going to whitewash this." He shook his head, a grim smile on his lips. "Dump the investigation on the boot lieutenant—that's you—then tell you how they want the mess cleaned up."

Dinah felt a surge of anger, the same anger she had felt when the executive officer put in his pitch for a report that concluded Slater's death was an accident. "Everyone keeps making assumptions about how I'm conducting this investigation. I was given a job to do. When I get the answers I'll call it the way I see it."

"Even if they hang you out to dry?" Bryce said, challenge in his voice.

"That won't happen." But it could, said a little unwelcome whisper in her head. She pushed the thought aside. "When was the last time you saw Slater?"

"That afternoon, right after she saw the captain."

"She saw the captain?"

"Sure. That's why she changed from her working uniform to her dress blues."

"I knew she wanted to talk to the CO. Chief Belsen said he told Slater to submit a request chit."

"Ginny told me about that, right before lunch. She said she'd wait until later that afternoon. Belsen usually disappears after lunch and Ginny said she checked Lorraine's calendar and Lorraine was leaving early for an appointment. She planned to walk in cold, see if the captain would talk to her. I figured that's what she did when I saw her coming out of the office."

"The captain's office or Lorraine's office?"

"Lorraine's office," Bryce said, "because she was just stepping into the corridor. But she must have seen the captain, because Lorraine wasn't there. Ginny looked upset. I think she was crying. She didn't answer when I called to her. It wasn't much later that she killed herself."

Hearsay, Dinah thought. Circumstantial. That's what her

lawyer husband would say. None of this is usable, hard evidence. Particularly since the Dragon Lady's statement to the base police contradicted what Bryce just told her.

"How did you know Lorraine wasn't there?"

"I saw her heading for the parking lot at two-thirty."

"What time did you see Slater in the hall outside the captain's office?"

"Between three and three-thirty. I went back to my office, then I left the building at a quarter to four and went to pick up some dry cleaning. I heard the sirens around four."

Dinah stared at the coffee growing cold in her cup, pondering the time lag between Bryce's last glimpse of Ginny Slater and the woman's death. Had Slater actually talked to the Dragon Lady? Surely if she had the captain would have mentioned such essential information in her statement to the base police. It was possible the captain hadn't even been in her office. But if Bryce was correct in his guess it meant there was a discrepancy in the Dragon Lady's story, a large one.

Suddenly she remembered that Lorraine had never called back Wednesday to let her know that the captain was available. And Dinah had been so busy today she hadn't thought about it until now.

Friday morning Dinah reminded Lorraine that she needed to speak with the captain. "I told her," the secretary protested. "Didn't she call you? She said she would."

"No. I'll go in now if she's here."

"Sorry, Lieutenant. She's at a conference in San Francisco. She may be out of the office all day."

"Monday, then." As Dinah left the office she felt an odd sense of relief at not having to deal with it today. She never relished her encounters with the Dragon Lady. Then Dinah felt annoyed and ashamed. Damn it, she told herself, I am not afraid of her.

That afternoon Dinah went to get a soda from the machine in the lounge. She reached to drop the coins into the slot, then jumped as the Dragon Lady's voice sawed through her mood, catching her off-guard.

"Where's that report, Lieutenant? It has to be submitted in a timely fashion."

Dinah's hand tightened on the coins as she dropped her hand to her side. "I'm still working on it, Captain. In fact, I want to ask—"

"Still working on it?" The Dragon Lady scowled. "You've been working on it all week. Dawdling over it, more likely. You don't need to interview every sailor who hoisted a beer with Slater. From what I can see it all looks cut and dried."

"Captain, I have to ask you some questions."

"You have the necessary statements and reports. That's all the information you need. Get with it, Lieutenant. I want that report written and on my desk first thing Monday morning."

The Dragon Lady marched down the hall toward her office, leaving Dinah with clenched hands and raw nerves. She shoved the coins into her pocket and walked back to her office. I am afraid of her, Dinah admitted. Afraid of what she can do to me, to my Navy career. Because she has power and I don't. All I have is a responsibility.

Friday afternoons the building always emptied quickly as people headed off in search of the weekend's pleasures. Dinah stayed at her desk, catching up on paperwork, trying to ignore the manila file folder containing the bits and pieces of her investigation. Finally she cleared off her desk and walked down the corridor to the office Slater had shared with several other petty officers. Her desk had been purged of personal items. Now it was just an available desk, ready for the next warm body.

Dinah pulled out the drawers and stared at the residue, paperclips and pencils adrift in one drawer, phone message pads and request chit forms in another. The top right drawer held a plastic insert with compartments. Here she saw pens, pencils, rubber bands and more paperclips. She pushed the drawer shut but it stuck halfway. She pushed, then pulled, but it wouldn't budge. Muttering under her breath, she tugged again and the drawer suddenly sailed out all the way. She caught it just as it was about to fall and carefully set it back on the track.

The insert had shifted and at the back of the drawer Dinah saw something hidden underneath, its corner now visible. Lifting the insert, Dinah saw a long white envelope. She pulled it out and turned it over as she shut the drawer. The envelope was addressed to Slater, with a Jacksonville postmark and the initials "JL" in the upper left corner. This must be the letter Bryce said Slater had received. He'd missed it in his cursory search of Slater's desk.

The envelope was slit at the top. Dinah removed two folded sheets of paper, one white and the other yellow. The white sheet had writing on both sides, and it was creased and crinkled from handling. As she read the words, Dinah understood the reason for Slater's spiraling depression. Bryce was right. Ginny Slater's officer from Guam was married. *It's over,* he wrote. *Don't call me, don't write me.* Dinah unfolded the yellow sheet and read Slater's unfinished reply, an anguished plea scrawled in black ink. *I still love you. I'll get a transfer, I'll get out of the Navy. I can't live without you . . .*

Dinah wrote the report in her head first, composing sentences as she took a long walk in the Berkeley hills, bundled up against a misty February rain, then warming herself in a café with a cup of cappuccino. The chain of command wouldn't like what she had to say, but she'd done her investigation by the book, her conclusions based on the evidence as well as her own gut feelings. Facts may be inconclusive, she told herself, but my stomach seldom is.

She worked late Saturday night, revising draft after draft before she was satisfied with a final version. Should she include Bryce's information about seeing Slater outside the captain's office? There was no hard evidence to indicate she had actually spoken with the Dragon Lady. Besides, she had Jeff's letter and Slater's unfinished reply to indicate the dead woman's mood. Finally she decided to omit that part of Bryce's statement. On Sunday afternoon she read her report again, wondering if she should change anything. No, she decided, closing the folder. It's the way it should be.

Dinah photocopied the report early Monday morning, then put the original on the captain's desk. As she slipped her copy into an envelope and tucked it into her briefcase, relief washed over her and she told herself, it's finished. But she didn't really believe that. Just before lunch the captain's secretary called to tell Lieutenant Gray that the commanding officer would like to see her.

"I've read your report," the Dragon Lady said abruptly, as soon as Dinah closed the door. The folder lay in the center of her desk. The captain looked at it as though it were ticking. "It's absolute nonsense. Where in the world did you get the idea Slater committed suicide?"

"My reasons are in the report," Dinah said, feeling like a schoolgirl called to the principal's office.

"I'm not impressed with your reasoning." The Dragon Lady leaned forward and drummed her fingers on the desk, a nervous tattoo that reminded Dinah of a drum roll. "Explain how you came up with this conclusion."

"Slater was depressed after she received the letter from her married boyfriend. Her reply indicates her state of mind. There was nothing wrong with the vehicle, according to the mechanic. Slater deliberately drove the car into the bay, at a high rate of speed and making no effort to stop. The witness says the window was down. Slater could have unfastened the seat belt and gotten out the window, but she made no attempt to save herself. That indicates suicide to me."

The Dragon Lady ticked her counterarguments off on her fingers. "The mechanic could be wrong about the car. After all, it was in the water for a number of hours. Slater could have been in shock. Or injured. And thus unable to swim to shore. As for her state of mind, you're reaching, Lieutenant."

"She was depressed about the breakup of a relationship and her inability to do anything about it."

"That's speculation on your part. Besides, these days it's ridiculous to assume a woman would kill herself over some man."

"People still feel hurt when rejected, captain. That doesn't change with the times."

"She didn't leave a suicide note. An unfinished letter to a friend hardly qualifies." The captain stood and walked to the window, looking out at the choppy bay water.

"She says she can't live without him."

The Dragon Lady dismissed Dinah's words with a wave of her hand. She walked to her desk, picked up the report and shoved it at Dinah. "This is unacceptable."

"You want me to change it," Dinah said, keeping her hands at her sides. She heard a roaring sound in her ears, like a train.

"I want you to reexamine your conclusions."

Dinah took a deep breath. "You asked me to conduct a JAG Manual investigation, Captain. I did so. I believe Slater committed suicide. My reasons for that conclusion are in the report. If you're asking me to change that report, I must respectfully decline."

The Dragon Lady had been in the Navy long enough to be adept at masking her emotions, but Dinah thought she saw a flicker of fury in the woman's cold blue eyes. One of your sailors killed herself on your watch, Dinah thought. That doesn't look good on your fitness reports. It makes that promotion board wonder whether you're admiral material.

The captain set the report on her desk with a thud. "That will be all, Lieutenant."

Dinah returned to her office, unsure what would happen next. Would the report go out? Would the Dragon Lady sit on it, or pressure Dinah to change her conclusions? A few days passed, and she heard nothing. I should have received a copy after it was signed, she thought, with growing disquiet. She walked down the hall to the administrative office. The report had gone out, the command yeoman told her, headed up through the chain of command to Washington. Certainly, she could see a copy. He pulled it out of a filing cabinet and handed it to Dinah. She read the first page and gasped, quickly leafing through the remaining pages.

"The exec is with her," the captain's secretary warned. Dinah ignored her. She walked straight into the dragon's lair, copy of the report in her hand. The captain was seated at her desk, while Commander Fox stood at her side, pointing out something on a chart. They looked up, startled. Then the Dragon Lady glanced at the exec, who gathered his chart and retreated, closing the door behind him.

"You changed it," Dinah said. She read the words, their meaning blurred by officialese. " 'The evidence is insufficient to determine whether the incident was accidental or deliberate.' That's not what I wrote. It's a lie. You sent it out over my signature."

"Sit down, Lieutenant." The captain's voice was as neutral as her expression.

"I'll stand, thank you. What did you do with Slater's letters? They aren't there, with the attachments."

The Dragon Lady didn't answer. She picked up her curved brass letter opener and fingered the point. "I can see now that you were the wrong person to conduct this investigation."

"Why? Because I call it as I see it?"

"You don't see it clearly. You let your emotions get in the way of your judgment. You're a young woman investigating the death of another young woman. Naturally you're sympathetic, looking for reasons where they don't exist." The Dragon Lady set the letter opener aside, her eyes devoid of anything but ice. "There is no conclusive evidence that Slater intended to kill herself. Yes, her car went into San Francisco Bay."

"Slater *drove* her car into the bay," Dinah interrupted. The woman talked like a Navy directive, as though no human hand had gripped the wheel. "It didn't go in by itself."

"But we don't know why and we never will." The Dragon Lady shook her head. "In the absence of some indication of Slater's intent, to submit a report commenting on the probability of her having committed suicide is irresponsible. Do you want to muddy the waters because of some romantic notion on your part? Think about Slater's family. How would they feel?"

"Those letters indicate her intent. But you deep-sixed them." Dinah heard the train roar in her ears again. Suddenly she wasn't afraid of the Dragon Lady anymore. "You're not the least bit concerned about Slater's family. You're covering your back. And I know why."

The captain narrowed her eyes. "What are you talking about?"

"Slater was seen coming out of your office, shortly before she killed herself."

"That's not in your report."

"I didn't put it in the report because I didn't have the opportunity to ask you about it. Each time I tried to see you, you were unavailable."

"So you wrote your report without interviewing me?" Dinah saw a smile twist one corner of the Dragon Lady's mouth. "That's very slipshod, Lieutenant. I'm astonished at your carelessness and laxity. It's just as well I edited it before sending it out."

"You were dodging me. Lorraine told you I wanted to ask you some questions about your statement, but you never called me, as you told her you would. When I saw you on Friday you told me I had all the information I needed. All the information you wanted me to have, you mean. You didn't want to talk about your meeting with Slater."

"I don't recall seeing Slater that afternoon." The captain's voice was cool, noncommittal, convincing in its calmness. But the errant smile played with her lips and she looked smug, like a supremely confident cat. "That's what I told the base police. I stand by my statement."

"I'll bet you do. But you're lying," Dinah said, provoked beyond caution. A junior lieutenant didn't talk that way to a captain, particularly the captain who signed her fitness reports. "Slater wanted a transfer and you turned her down. Probably with your usual flair for making people feel two inches tall."

The captain's ladylike façade slipped and Dinah saw the dragon. She placed her hands on her desk and stood up, towering over Dinah. Her eyes burned with a cold flame that belied the deliberate calm of her words.

"Lieutenant, you're behaving irrationally, making wild

194

accusations. Apologize immediately and leave my office. And understand that your next fitness report will reflect what I consider to be your complete lack of qualification to be an officer."

Dinah laughed, fuel to the fire in the captain's eyes. "If you're going to trash me anyway it doesn't matter what I say. So I'll say it and you'll just have to listen." Dinah felt a giddy, heedless freedom, a power she that came with not caring what happened now.

"You set me up. You dumped that investigation on me for the same reason you accuse me of having romantic notions. Because I'm a woman. You thought you could manipulate me. You thought another woman would do it the way you wanted. Then you made sure I wouldn't get the facts, because you're the only one who has them. When I didn't come through with the desired result, you tried intimidation, then you changed my report. It won't do you any good. I kept a copy of the report for my files. Including Slater's letters. You didn't think of that, did you? What if I send a copy of my original to your superior?"

"Your rough draft means nothing," the Dragon Lady hissed. "The only report that matters is the one that went to Washington with my signature on it."

"But you'll know that copy's out there," Dinah said, thankful she'd taken the file home. She wouldn't put it past the captain to pull a raid on her files here at the command. "And you'll know that I know the truth. What did you tell Slater, when she came in here that day and pleaded with you for a transfer? When you saw how desperate and disturbed she was? Not that it mattered to you. People don't matter, or their feelings."

"Feelings. Emotions." The Dragon Lady's voice was edged with contempt. "They get in the way. I've been in the Navy a long time, Lieutenant, butting heads against the old

195

boys' network since you were in rompers. Nobody cut me any slack. I had to work hard and be twice as good as any man. The only way to get four gold stripes on your sleeve, a command and a shot at making admiral is to jettison things like feelings. I can't cater to the whim of every lovelorn little girl who comes in here whimpering because some man did her wrong."

"You did see her. She didn't measure up to your requirements for the new Navy woman, so you tossed her overboard. Not everyone can be as strong or as cold as you." Poor Ginny Slater. She deserved more than the Dragon Lady's deceit.

"Hearsay. You can't prove it."

"I don't have to prove it," Dinah said, leaning toward the captain. "The implication will be enough to interest the admirals in Washington. And certainly the press. How would you like to have some investigative reporter asking tough questions you can't answer?"

The arrow hit bull's-eye and the Dragon Lady paled. "You wouldn't dare," she snapped. Then she squared her shoulders and tilted her chin. "Who do you think they'll believe? Me or you? A senior captain with twenty-five years in the Navy, or a misfit, insubordinate lieutenant?"

"Do you really want to take that chance?" Dinah walked to the door and opened it. "I don't fit your image either, Captain. I think people are as important as the mission. By the way, if you make any formal charges of insubordination against me, we'll have to explain why. I don't think you want to risk that."

As Dinah left the office the Dragon Lady bellowed, loud enough to turn the heads of everyone within range of her voice. Dinah smiled to herself and pushed through the people in the hall, flying the tattered shreds of her Navy career like a flag over a flaming bridge.

"What the Cat Dragged In" appeared in the anthology Cat Crimes Through Time. *The Gold Rush town of Cibola nestles in a little valley between San Andreas and Mokelumne Hill. I can see it, but it doesn't exist, except in the pages of fiction. I created Cibola for an unfinished historical novel, one I may finish yet. Then I used it as a setting in my first Jeri Howard novel,* Kindred Crimes. *An imaginary town is a useful place. I can create the scenery, arrange the buildings, and write the history to suit my purpose. I may revisit Cibola again, as I did in this story about a cat, a woman gold miner in California's Mother Lode and the Foreign Miners' Tax of 1850.*

What the Cat Dragged In

The tiger-striped cat appeared at the edge of the clearing one afternoon while Hattie Ballew was chopping wood. Hattie's brothers, Ned and Tom, had gone hunting, for the same reason Hattie labored at the woodpile. They needed plenty of fuel and game stored before autumn gave way to winter. Snow had already fallen in the upper elevations of the Sierra Nevada. Days were shorter, and the nights had turned chilly.

Perhaps that was why the cat showed up, seeking more comfortable quarters. To be sure, she looked scrawny, her ribs showing under the brown and black fur. She meowed, beseeching Hattie for something to eat.

The need for a cat came on Hattie, as sharp as the big ax she'd been hefting. It would be nice, she told herself, to have something soft and warm to doze in her lap in the evening.

Hattie set down the ax and went inside the cabin. She scraped the leavings from the pan of stew they'd had at midday into a chipped crockery bowl and carried it back outside. The cat waited at the edge of the clearing. Hattie set the bowl down on the ground, then backed off and watched. The cat didn't hesitate. Hunger propelled her toward the bowl, where she consumed every scrap. Then she sat back, pink tongue darting as she licked the residue from the fur around her mouth. The expectant look in her wide green eyes, followed by another meow, told Hattie the cat was waiting for more.

"Got no more," Hattie told the cat. "Not now, anyhow.

But you stick with me, Little Bit. Maybe we'll both strike it rich."

Little Bit wasn't so little anymore. With the onset of winter and regular eating, her coat became thick and full, the sleek brown showing only her black stripes, not her ribs. She slept with Hattie on the crude rawhide bed with its mattress stuffed with straw, both of them curled into tight balls against the winter cold that seeped in through the cabin's log walls. During the days, Hattie and her brothers worked their claim. Ned and Tom used pickax and shovel to loosen the earth along the creek's banks, while Hattie shoveled the resultant dirt and gravel into the rocker and poured water over it, using the apparatus to sift through and search for the glittering bits of gold.

While the Ballews worked, Little Bit sunned herself on a flat stone near the rocker. Or she'd go off into the woods to stalk small animals and birds. Sometimes, when she caught something, the cat would haul it back to the cabin to display her trophy.

"Look what the cat dragged in now!" Hattie cried many an evening as she was greeted by a half-eaten jay or the fluffy tail of a squirrel.

Little Bit was certainly one for dragging things all over creation, and more often than not it was out of the cabin as well as in. Once, Hattie saw the cat trotting into the woods carrying an apple core that Ned had tossed away. Another time it was one of Tom's thick woolen socks, which Hattie had retrieved before the cat disappeared into the woods. Hattie figured Little Bit had a place out in the woods where she hid the things she had taken.

"If we're not careful, she'll thieve our gold," Hattie told her brothers, so the Ballews took care to hide away their bags of dust and nuggets, lest the cat find one and drag it to

Kingdom Come, spilling out the result of all their labors.

They hadn't struck it rich yet, not like some of the others working the Mother Lode. But they weren't busted either. They'd found plenty of color in the stream running through her claim, enough to keep them, and Little Bit, in food, enough to send some home to the folks, enough to keep their hopes alive.

The creek was called Cibola, just like the town that had sprung up on its banks, in a sloping valley between the Mokelumne and Calaveras Rivers. If you could call that rough mining camp a town. It sure didn't look like the towns Hattie was used to, back in Missouri. Cibola had been thrown together from tents and lumber in the spring of 1849, when the world, lured by the seductive promise of gold, rushed into California.

Early in 1848, a man named James Marshall found gold at Sutter's Mill on the American River. Gold fever spread up and down California and into Northern Mexico. It wasn't until later that year that the news filtered back east. In August there was a story in a St. Louis newspaper, and that folded piece of newsprint came back to the Ballew farm in the back pocket of Pa's britches.

"Well, I'm going to California," Hattie declared when she'd read the story. "Get me a pile of gold and live like a queen."

"I never heard the like," Ma said with a snort as she dished up bowls of stew and handed them around the table. "You're not going to California."

"Yes, I am. What do you mean, you never heard the like?" Hattie folded her arms across her chest and squared her jaw. "Why, the Ballews have always been fiddlefooted, and the MacNeills too." She turned to her father. "Wasn't it you who walked all the way from Virginia to Kentucky, through the Cumberland Gap?"

"That's a fact." Pa nodded, sucking on his pipe.

Now Hattie looked at her mother. "And wasn't it your grandparents who came across the ocean a hundred years ago, without any idea of what might lie ahead?"

"They knew what was in back of them," Ma said. "English soldiers, after anyone who'd fought on the side of the Bonnie Prince." She frowned at Hattie, her eldest. "But that was different. They were families, not unmarried girls, all on their own."

"She won't be all on her own," Ned piped up from the other side of the table. Tom was at his side, mouth full of cornbread, and both boys had eagerness flashing in their eyes. "We aim to go to California too. We can look after Hattie."

"Look after me? I never heard such nonsense." Hattie glared at her younger brothers over the table. "It was me taught the two of you how to shoot. I can look after myself, without the pair of you under my feet."

Pa threw his head back and laughed. "She can, at that. I'd bet on it."

"That's not all you'd bet on." Ma shook her head in exasperation. "Land sakes, the gold fever's got all of them." Ma reached for Hattie's strong brown hands, and cradled them in her smaller, work-roughened fingers. "I'd hoped you might marry Dan Cullen. He's been courting you this summer."

"Oh, Ma," Hattie said. "He's a nice enough feller. But I'm not ready to settle down. I won't be twenty till next spring."

The Ballews argued about it all winter. But come April of 1849, Hattie, Ned and Tom set out for Independence, where they joined a party of goldseekers heading overland to California. It was a hard trip that took them four months, but they made it.

When they found Cibola, there was nothing in the little valley but the creek and two miners digging for gold along its banks. The one who had arrived just a week earlier and staked his claim on the north side was a tall Kentuckian named Jack Murdock. He was a handsome, well-spoken fellow, Hattie thought, with his blue eyes and a head of curly black hair over a handlebar mustache and a full beard.

The one whose claim stretched on the creek's south bank had been there longer, a month or so. He, too, was pleasant to look at, dark eyes in a brown face and a wiry muscular figure. "My name is Miguel Santos," he told the Ballews. "I am from Sonora."

"The town farther south?" Hattie asked.

"No, *señorita*." Santos tipped his sombrero and bowed as though she were a great lady instead of a rawboned farm girl from Missouri with a battered straw hat atop her lank brown hair, riding a horse astride and decked out comfortably in Ned's shirt and trousers and a pair of Tom's old boots. "The state of Sonora, in Mexico. There are so many of my countrymen here in California that they named the town for us."

She smiled at Santos, who grinned back, his eyes sparkling up at her as he stood leaning on his shovel. "I like the look of this place," Hattie told her brothers. "Let's scout up that crick, and find us a claim."

The Ballews went farther upstream, a half mile or so, and staked a claim on the south side of the creek. They built a cabin with one big central room and two sleeping rooms on either side, one for Hattie and the other for the boys.

Cibola grew quickly as summer wound into fall, once word got out that there was color in the stream. Gold there was, glittering in the crevices along the twisting creek. The Ballews didn't find lumps as big as their hands, but they did all right. That's what she told her mother and father and the young'uns in the monthly letters she wrote by candlelight, snug that winter. They bought a small cookstove and a rocking chair, and it felt good on a winter's night to sit by the stove with Little Bit in her lap, Hattie's hands stroking the tiger cat's fur, feeling the vibration as the cat purred, listening as Ned played the fiddle and Tom picked his banjo. Sometimes their neighbors would join in, Miguel Santos with a guitar and, more infrequently, Jack Murdock playing the harmonica.

"Why did you name the place Cibola?" she asked Miguel, one afternoon in the spring of 1850. She'd come to town for supplies. Now she and Miguel stood in what passed for a store, a flimsy structure built of planks and canvas. "Been meaning to ask you that, all winter. You could have named the place after yourself, since you was the first to stake a claim here."

Miguel didn't answer her right away. He frowned as he read the front page of a copy of the *Alta California*, the newspaper published in San Francisco.

Hattie glared at the shopkeeper who was making money hand over fist by charging miners what the market would bear. "Land sakes, what they're charging for eggs! You'd think they was lumps of gold. I've a mind to get me some laying hens." But she wanted eggs, to make a cake for Ned's birthday, so she watched the shopkeeper like a hawk as the man weighed out the necessary gold dust for her purchase.

Miguel set the newspaper on the counter and turned to her. "My dear Hattie, have you not heard of the Seven Cities of Gold?"

"Not a word." Hattie wrapped her eggs carefully and put them in the basket she carried over one arm. "Are they somewhere near here?"

"They do not exist, as far as I know," the Sonoran said as

they left the store. He took her arm and steered her away from a group of rowdy, rough-clad men who'd spilled out the doors of a nearby saloon. "If they do exist, I suppose California is as good a place as any. The Seven Cities of Gold are a legend, and Cibola is one of them. Coronado searched the Southwest for them, but didn't find gold." Miguel laughed. "Unlike those of us who journeyed to California. There is an old Spanish fable about California. It's supposed to be an island paradise, full of gold and precious stones, ruled by the Amazon queen Calafia."

"What nonsense." Hattie shook her head as she surveyed Cibola's only street, rutted and muddy from the tail-end of the winter's rain. A man rode by on a mule, its hooves kicking up mud that soiled Hattie's trousers and shirt and splashed on her chin. Hattie scrubbed at the splotches on her bosom, making the mess worse. She gave up and looked at Miguel. "Does this look like an island paradise?"

"Perhaps not." Miguel took out one of the linen handkerchiefs he always carried. He used it to brush away the mud on her chin. Hattie looked at the initials "MS" embroidered on the corner and wondered if they'd been stitched there by Miguel's sweetheart back in Mexico. She'd never asked him. "California is not an island, as the legend promised," he continued. "But the gold is here. We just have to dig for it. And you, Hattie, perhaps you are the Amazon queen Calafia, here to wrest the gold from the earth."

Hattie's face turned red from the chin to the roots of her drab brown hair. "What nonsense," she said again, her voice roughened to hide her embarrassment. Why, she felt such a fool when he talked like that.

Hattie knew it seemed strange to people that an unmarried woman like her was in these mountains, working a claim. There were other women in the rough mining camps of the

Mother Lode, married to miners, some even working the claims with their husbands. Others ran boardinghouses and shops, cooked for the miners or took in washing. There were other kinds of women too, the ones people called soiled doves. But the men by far outnumbered the women. A lot of them wanted to get married, if only to have someone cook and clean for them, Hattie thought. She'd fended off men ever since she'd hit the Overland Trail for California. And more since she'd arrived, much to the amusement of her brothers, who couldn't fathom why anyone would want to hitch up with their sister.

The marriage proposals she dealt with easily enough, with a shake of the head and a firm "no," or even more words from a tart tongue if that became necessary. That was all it took to discourage Patch Turner, the red-faced Pennsylvanian who'd staked a claim about a mile south of town. He'd made a play for Hattie right after he got to Cibola, but she'd put him in his place smartly enough. As for the other sort of advances, she had a Colt revolver and a shotgun, and she knew how to use both.

Not that Hattie would have minded if Miguel came courting. He was a fine looking man, educated, with good manners, who managed to keep cleaner than most, and he always treated her like she was a lady, even if she hadn't worn a skirt since she left Missouri.

It was Patch Turner who told her the news, hailing her that April afternoon as she walked back up the creek to her cabin. He was at the edge of a knot of miners, wearing the colorful patched vest with brass buttons that gave him his nickname. She saw Jack Murdock, and Shorty LaRue, the Cajun from the Louisiana bayous, and a couple of Iowa farm boys, Johnny and Pete Brubaker.

"Did you hear about the tax?" Patch said as he hailed her.

"What tax?" She kept her distance. She didn't much like Patch, and she didn't want anyone to jostle her market basket and those expensive eggs.

"Why, the territorial legislature's passed a tax," Patch declared, moping his florid face with a dirty gray handkerchief. "Against the foreigners. About damn time, too. The damn Mexes and Chinee coolies are thick as flies, outnumbering the Americans. Taking gold that rightly belongs to Americans."

"Gold don't belong to nobody till it's found," Hattie said sharply. "And it don't matter to me who finds it."

Patch was talking nonsense. There were all sorts of people here in California and she liked it fine that way. Plenty of people had come from back east, like the Ballews. There were lots of Mexicans, like Miguel, and she'd once met a fellow from a place called Peru, way down in South America. There was an Englishman up in Mokelumne Hill, a bagpipe-playing Scot in San Andreas, and an Australian down in Angel's Camp. She herself had met a Frenchwoman who, with her husband, worked a claim in Fiddletown. And the Chinese in their strange pigtails were a familiar sight in all the rough towns up and down the Mother Lode.

"Some don't agree with you," Murdock told Hattie, his deep voice slow and carrying the flavor of his Southern roots, as well as evidence of his education. "The legislature's decreed that only native or naturalized citizens of the United States will be permitted to mine in California, without a license, that is. All foreign miners must have a license, which costs twenty dollars a month."

"Twenty dollars!" Hattie's eyes widened with astonishment at the figure. "Why, that's . . . that's . . ."

"A princely sum," Murdock finished. "It will drive a lot of them away."

"Sounds like a damn fool notion to me," Hattie said, regaining her composure. "What if they won't pay it?"

"There'll be trouble," Patch said, with a laugh, almost as though he relished the thought. The Brubakers joined in.

There was already trouble in the Mother Lode. Shootings, stabbings, robberies and even murders were common in the mines, as the hordes of goldseekers competed for the glitter that drew them to California. Hattie heard Americans blaming the Mexicans for these crimes, but from what she could see in Cibola and the other towns she visited, troublemakers came in all nationalities.

"Truth be told," she said to Little Bit when she returned to the cabin, "there's too damn many of us, scratching for gold all over these mountains."

Little Bit paid her no mind. The tiger cat was dragging an item of clothing from Hattie's room into the main room of the cabin, heading, no doubt, out the door to her cache. Hattie left her basket on the table and rescued her last clean pair of underdrawers, not so clean now that the cat had been at them. She shook them free of dust and hung them on a peg near her bed, then returned to the main room, removing her precious cargo of eggs from the basket.

She remembered how it was last year when she and her brothers had arrived on the banks of Cibola Creek, just the three of them, Jack Murdock and Miguel Santos. Now there were hundreds crowding the little valley. If she multiplied that by the number of gold camps scattered throughout the Mother Lode . . . She stopped, shook her head, and spoke again to the cat, who'd jumped up on the table and was eyeing those eggs. "Don't you dare, Little Bit." Hattie moved the eggs out of danger. "Why, there must be thousands more in the diggings than there were last year. When you get that many people crowded together, there's likely to be trouble."

There was.

She heard about it from her brothers, who'd been in Sonora when it happened. The foreign miners, outraged by the tax, refused to pay it. Several thousand of them gathered and paraded through Sonora. In response, several hundred American miners organized an armed force.

There was a murder, Ned told Hattie. Maybe two, Tom chimed in, and a few arrests. After this conflict, an uneasy peace settled over the Mother Lode. In the camps on the pages of the newspapers, arguments about the Foreign Miners' Tax continued.

"What do you think of this tax?" Hattie asked Miguel at his claim, a few days after the Sonora incident.

He'd been digging with his pickax and now he stopped, mopping his brow with one of his monogrammed handkerchiefs. "All of California used to belong to Mexico, until the Bear Flaggers took over Sonoma in 1846, and the *Americanos* occupied Monterey. My cousin Juan and his family have a rancho near San Luis Obispo. They are old *Californios,* who have been here for more than a hundred years. Why should we be called foreigners? It wasn't so long ago that people from the United States were foreigners."

"I know," Hattie said. "But Sonora ain't the last of it. Some Chinese miners up at Angel's Camp got burned out last night. I heard Patch Turner and those Brubaker boys spouting off about it when I was in town just now. They were sayin' all the foreigners better get out of Mother Lode."

"Especially 'the Mexes and the Chinee coolies.' And if we don't, Patch will do for all of us." Miguel shook his head. "Ah, Hattie, there are too many of us. Those three are blowhards. Get a little whiskey in them and they'll say anything."

She reckoned he was right, as she walked home. But all the time Patch and the others had been laughing about the fire that burned out the Chinese miners, she'd wondered if they'd been responsible for setting the blaze. When she heard the next day that Pete Brubaker took over the claim the Chinese had abandoned, she was convinced that they had.

The following Monday, Hattie rose later than usual. The boys had already made mush for breakfast, leaving cornmeal all over the table. But where was the letter she'd been writing to her mother? She'd left it right here, folded into a neat square and tucked into the addressed envelope. Perhaps Ned or Tom had taken it to town, where miners left letters at the store to be picked up each month by an expressman, who then took it to the post office in Sacramento, the first stop in the mail's long journey to San Francisco, then by steamer to Panama. But the expressman wasn't due in Cibola until tomorrow.

She reached for a rag to wipe the cornmeal off the table, then stopped when she saw the paw prints. "Little Bit. I'll be bound. That cat's dragged off my letter."

Hattie walked upstream to where her brothers were working the claim. "About time you got here, Miss Slug-A-Bed," Ned joshed. "You were sleeping so sound you didn't hear us getting our own breakfast."

"Must have been, since you make considerable noise most of the time." She turned to include Tom in her gaze. "Did you take that letter I was writing to Ma?"

"No," Tom said. "It was there on the table when we left."

"It's gone now. Had to be Little Bit, then." She didn't know whether to laugh or grumble.

Ned grinned. "If you find her, maybe you'll find that tobacco pouch I lost in March."

Hattie crossed to the north bank of the creek and walked

downstream to where Jack Murdock was sifting dirt, gravel and water into a rocker, staring intently at the contents as he looked for gold. "You seen Little Bit?" she asked.

He looked up. "Your cat? No, I haven't."

She'd never known Little Bit to wander as far as Cibola, so she crossed the creek again and headed for Miguel's cabin. Before she reached it she came on Patch Turner, digging a trench, a pickax in his meaty hands.

"What are you doing on Miguel's claim?" she demanded.

"Why, howdy, Miss Hattie," he said cheerfully. He stopped digging and leaned on the shovel, taking a cigar from the pocket of his disreputable patchwork vest. He ought to give the thing a good wash, Hattie thought, wrinkling her nose in disgust. Why, it's greasy and torn. There's a button missing and a corner's been ripped off that patch of red and yellow calico.

"I asked you a question," she said.

"And not very polite at that. This ain't Miguel's claim any more. It's mine."

She put her hands on her hips and glared at Patch. "What have you done with Miguel?"

"Done nothin' with him. He upped and left last night. The claim's abandoned, so I'm takin' it."

"Abandoned." She shook her head in disbelief. "He wouldn't do that. He was the first one to stake a claim in this valley. Besides, he wouldn't leave without telling me."

"Well, he's gone for sure. Johnny Brubaker saw him riding out of town, heading south. No doubt he's gone back to Mexico where he belongs."

"I don't believe it," Hattie said. She wouldn't believe either of the Brubakers if those boys swore the sun came up in the east.

"Suit yourself," Patch told her, and went back to digging.

211

Hattie left off her search for the cat and walked into Cibola. Sure enough, Johnny Brubaker told the tale as Patch Turner had described. He swore he'd seen Miguel Santos pack up all his belongings and ride south.

"It's not like him," Jack Murdock said later, when all three of the Ballews walked down to where he was working, to share the news. "Without a word. I can't believe Miguel would just leave."

"He hasn't left," Hattie said grimly. "Someone's kilt him. I'll be bound if it's not Patch Turner who's kilt Miguel for his claim."

Tom shook his head slowly. "Better watch your tongue, Sister, before you accuse a man of killing someone."

"That's right," Ned agreed. "I didn't hear any shots in the night."

"Even if it is true, how could you prove such a thing?" Murdock sat down on a stump and stretched his long legs in front of him. "Granted, no one's seen Miguel, but it's possible he left. A lot of the foreign miners have been driven away by the tax."

"Or by other miners," Hattie said, thinking of the Chinese who'd been burned out.

"I'll ride south tomorrow," Ned told her. "As far as San Andreas. To see if anyone saw Miguel. I can take Ma's letter into town when I go."

Hattie'd forgotten all about the letter, when she'd heard the news that Miguel was gone. Now she remembered. The fool cat had made off with the letter and she'd gone looking for it, which was why she was out tramping around instead of helping her brothers work the claim. She walked with them back up to the Ballew claim, then set off into the woods to the south, calling and whistling for Little Bit. She found herself circling to the west, coming out behind Miguel's cabin. She didn't see anything that would contradict Patch Turner's claim that Miguel had simply left Cibola.

Hattie turned and headed back toward the Ballew cabin. When she'd walked a few yards, movement caught her eye. A squirrel? No, it was Little Bit, looking smug and satisfied with herself as she trotted into view from behind a clump of boulders. The cat had something white in her mouth.

"My letter," Hattie cried. She grabbed for it, but the cat eluded her, thinking she was playing a game. Little Bit took off, her prize clamped firmly in her jaws, heading uphill through the pines and oak. Hattie ran after her, puffing from the exertion, in time to see the cat disappear into the gnarled tangle of some tree roots.

"Come on, Little Bit," she wheedled. "You know Ma and Pa and the young'uns look forward to those letters." Hattie got down on all fours and crept closer to the trees. As she got closer, she saw the earth had washed out from under the roots, forming a small cave. Here Little Bit had stashed her treasures. Hattie saw Ned's tobacco pouch, just as he'd predicted, as well as a brass button, the bowl of someone's corn cob pipe, assorted bones and bits of fur. Little Bit dropped the white scrap on top of this mound and settled down, paws tucked under her and her green eyes glittering. She looked pleased with herself.

Hattie reached in, her fingers searching for the letter. Little Bit hissed at her indignantly. Hattie pulled her hand away, but what she held didn't feel like paper.

Hattie stared down in alarm. It was part of a handkerchief, torn raggedly in half, stained with dirt and something brown and stiff. Was it dried blood? The monogram in one corner told her that it belonged to Miguel Santos.

She reached again into Little Bit's cave, ignoring the paw that swiped at her, and pulled out the brass button. It had a string of white thread clinging to it. Hadn't Patch Turner's vest been missing a button when she saw him earlier today? She tried to recall if the buttons on his vest had been sewed with white thread.

She got to her feet. Jack Murdock and her brothers would say this proved nothing. Miguel Santos was still missing, and Little Bit could have gotten these things anywhere. The cat was notorious for her thieving ways. But where had she found the handkerchief and the button?

Hattie whirled and went back the way she'd come, searching for the boulders where she'd first seen the cat. There it was, some fifty feet from the back of Miguel's cabin. She heard voices coming from inside the cabin as she crept around the big rocks. Sounded like Patch Turner and the Brubaker boys, drinking whiskey early this afternoon.

Behind the rocks Hattie found a gully. It looked as though someone had been dumping dirt and gravel here, the leavings from working a claim. One spot looked as though something had been digging at the pile, probably Little Bit. The cat had followed her back to this spot. With a proprietary meow, Little Bit poked a paw at the place where she'd been digging earlier. Hattie knelt and scrabbled at the dirt with her hands.

When she saw the cold stiff hands, one of them clenched, she recoiled. Then with renewed urgency, she brushed away more dirt until she saw Miguel's dead face and his chest with the blood-caked wound where he'd been stabbed. Hattie gritted her teeth and peered closer, trying to see what was hidden in Miguel's hand.

Quick as a wink, Little Bit's paw reached out. One claw snagged the edge of a piece of cloth and teased it from the dead man's closed fingers. Before the cat could run away, Hattie grabbed her by the scruff and pried the cloth away from her. It was red and yellow calico. Hattie knew where she'd seen the pattern before.

Quickly she covered the body again, then got to her feet, shooing Little Bit ahead of her as she moved quickly through the woods, toward the Ballew cabin. Tom and Ned were there, washing up outside the front door.

"Where have you been?" Ned called. "We found the letter. It was on the floor under our bed. Looks like Little Bit knocked it off the table and played with it. She chewed on it some. You're lucky she didn't drag it into the woods, or you'd never find it."

He and Tom laughed. Then they stopped when they saw the look on their sister's face. Hattie reached into her pocket. She pulled out the button, the calico scrap and the handkerchief that held Miguel's initials and the stains from his wound.

"Look what the cat dragged in."

"Invisible Time" appeared in the anthology Once Upon a Crime. *One afternoon while in a San Francisco bakery, I noticed a homeless man hovering in the doorway. I knew from his body language that he was planning to steal something. As I watched, he took a bag of cookies from a nearby display. Later, when asked to write a story with a fairy tale theme, the tale of Hansel and Gretel immediately came to mind. My homeless children, Hank and Greta, are lost in the very mean urban forest of San Francisco, where they encounter modern-day evils. But in the end, resilient and resourceful, they survive.*

Invisible Time

Greta watched the front door of the bakery on Geary Street, choosing her moment. When it came, it was brought by a middle-aged woman who wore a business suit and running shoes.

The woman stopped at the window, eyed the tempting display of cakes, cookies and breads, then moved toward the door. Greta slipped up behind the woman, a pace back from the leather briefcase that swung from her left hand. The woman pushed open the door, her entry ringing the bell above the door.

The bakery clerk was a gangly young man wearing a silly white paper hat perched on his brown hair. He looked up from his post behind the counter and smiled at the woman. He didn't see Greta.

Fine. That's what she had in mind. Now that she was inside, Greta hovered near the door, keeping one eye on the grown-ups and the other eye on the bakery's wares. Picking a target was tough. The goods were piled alluringly on counters and shelves and stand-alone displays. Finally she spotted her best shot, bags of day-old cookies mounded high in a basket at the edge of a low table, just a few steps from the door that led out to the busy sidewalk.

The bakery clerk's head was down. He was busy boxing up a cake for a customer, a big man with a fat belly. Looked like he got plenty to eat, Greta told herself as she edged closer to the basket. Unlike some people she could name.

The customer Greta had followed into the bakery stood on the other side of the table, examining the loaves of day-old bread stacked there as she waited her turn at the counter. She hummed to herself and tapped one finger on the edge of the basket that held the cookies. Greta kept her head down, her blue eyes constantly shifting as she observed the bakery's occupants. The woman moved closer. Greta thought she smelled good, like flowers, but she didn't smell as good as the combined perfume of what came out of the bakery's ovens.

Handing the clerk a twenty, the big man put a proprietary hand on top of the box containing his cake. While the clerk looked down at the drawer of the cash register, Greta snaked her hand toward the cookies. She grabbed two bags, whirled and made for the door.

"Hey, little girl," the woman in running shoes said, sounding surprised and shocked as she moved to stop this theft in progress. The little girl shoved the woman hard, knocking her into the table, and kept going, darting past a trio of teenagers who'd just opened the bakery door wide, giving Greta an open shot to freedom.

Once she was out on the sidewalk she dodged to the right and ran up Geary Street, against the tide of pedestrians heading down toward Market Street, where BART and the San Francisco Municipal Railway would take them home. Intent on their own destinations, they took no notice of the skinny little girl in baggy blue jeans and a red sweatshirt, her dirty blond hair spilling to her shoulders.

Hank was waiting for her in Union Square, on the side close to the entrance to the Saint Francis Hotel and the cable cars that clanged up and down Powell Street. At his feet was a brown nylon bag with a zipper and a shoulder strap. It contained everything they owned—clothes, a couple of beat-up stuffed animals, and a picture of Mom.

"You get something?" he asked eagerly, brown eyes too big in his pinched face. He looked far more streetwise than a five-year-old boy should.

"Yeah. Cookies. Two bags. Looks like one of 'em is chocolate chip and the other is maybe oatmeal raisin. Did you get anything?"

"Pizza," he said triumphantly, displaying a dented cardboard box. "With pepperoni. Some guy was sitting on that bench over there eating it, and he didn't eat it all. He was gonna throw it in the trash. But he saw me watching him, so he gave it to me. Look, there's two whole pieces left."

"All right!" They high-fived it.

Then they hunkered down on the bench to eat their booty. People hurrying through the square paid no mind to the two children, any more than they did to the pigeons congregating around the statue of *Victory* atop the column in the center of the square. As she ate, Greta watched shoppers laden with bags scurry from store to store. Hank focused on the food with the single-minded appetite of a little boy who never gets enough to eat.

The store windows in Macy's and Saks were full of glittering decorations, red, green, gold and silver, signaling the approaching holiday season, and there was a big lighted Christmas tree in the square. But the passage of time meant little to Greta. She only knew that the days were shorter than they had been. The sunshine, what little there was of it, had turned thin and weak. Nights were longer and it was harder for her and her brother to stay warm. Today the wind had turned cold. From what little she could see of the late afternoon sky, it was dark gray.

It was going to rain, she was sure of it. She didn't know what they'd do if it rained. They'd been sleeping in doorways and alleys all over the downtown area, constantly moving so the cops wouldn't find them during their periodic sweeps to rid the streets of human litter.

If it rains we'll have to go inside somewhere, Greta told herself. But it wasn't safe to go down inside the BART station to spend the night. The BART cops would catch them. And there were too many weirdos down there already. Mom had always told Greta to take care of her little brother and to stay away from the weirdos.

She was doing the best she could, but she didn't know how long she could keep it up. She was careful to limit their range to the Union Square area, north of Market Street. That's where the nice stores, restaurants and hotels were. Greta felt safer where the people were better dressed. Sometimes those people gave them money, or food, like Hank's pizza bene-factor. South of Market and the Tenderloin were different, full of run-down buildings and scary people who would take their stuff, even during the day, though it was more dan-gerous after dark.

Greta couldn't remember when Mom left. A few weeks, a month, two months, it didn't matter. After a few days, the hours all ran together, like a stream of dirty water chasing debris down the sewer grate. She only remembered that it didn't used to be like this.

Once she'd had a father, though lately it was hard to recall what he'd looked like. They'd lived in a nice apartment, two bedrooms so Greta had a room of her own. She had a baby doll and a crib her dad had made for her, pretty dresses. She remembered all of this. Or maybe she thought she remem-bered, because Mom had told her.

She knew that one day her father hadn't come home. Although it was a long time ago, she remembered that day and the days afterward quite clearly. Mom crying, people bringing food to the apartment. They talked about God's will and a car crash. Greta didn't understand how or why God could have fixed it so that her father never came home, but no one bothered to explain it to her. She only knew that Mom missed him something terrible.

That was about the time Greta started kindergarten. Mom had a job working a cash register at some store, but it didn't pay much. Not enough to make ends meet, Mom told Greta. At the time Greta wasn't sure what that meant, but now that the ends didn't meet at all, she knew. That was when she and Mom went to live with Grandma.

Greta didn't much like Grandma. The old woman seemed as ancient as a dinosaur, and not even half as cuddly as the stuffed stegosaurus her mom had given her. Grandma coughed a lot and smelled bad, puffing on foul-smelling cigarettes even if she did have some sickness with a long name. She had a sharp tongue on her, too, one she used to peel layers off Greta's mom, until Mom didn't have much spirit left.

Then Mom met Hank's dad and got some of the sparkle back in her eyes. Of course, Grandma kicked them out because Mom took up with Hank's dad. He was a different color than Mom, and Grandma said bad things about him, but Greta liked him a lot. He drove a cab and brought her chocolate, her favorite. And when Hank was born, a year or so later, she thought the baby was beautiful. She loved him and swore she'd always take care of him, no matter what. She just didn't think it would be this soon.

Hank didn't remember his dad much. He was not quite three when the cab driver was shot to death. Greta heard one of the other cabbies at the funeral say Hank's dad should have given the money to the punk who pulled a gun on him late one night. But Greta figured maybe the punk would have shot him anyway.

Hank's dad had left something called life insurance, which was kind of strange to Greta, seeing he was dead. She'd have rather had Hank's dad instead of money. It hadn't been much anyway, and after a while there wasn't any left.

She was nine and in the fourth grade when Hank's dad got killed. She liked school, but the rest of her life was hard. She had to take care of Hank and Mom both. Hank because he was just a toddler, and Mom, because she was drinking, cheap sweet-smelling wine in big bottles. Greta would come home from school and find her passed out on the bed of the tiny apartment, Hank roaming around on the floor with soiled pants.

Greta stayed home from school more often, missing classes. No one ever seemed to notice she was gone. Mom got fired from her job at the store and didn't bother to get another one. She said she'd rather die than go back to live with Grandma, but as it turned out, Grandma had died by then and left all her money to some cousin.

They were evicted from that apartment. They moved to a run-down rickety hotel in the Tenderloin, where all three of them shared one room and a bath. Greta stopped going to school altogether, because looking after Mom and Hank was a full-time job. She'd cook their meager meals on a hot plate, put Mom to bed when she drank too much, and read to Hank so he could at least learn his letters. Then she'd put Hank to bed and try to get some sleep herself, which was hard to do. Down on the street, music spilled from the bars and the hookers called to men cruising by in cars. The hookers worked for a tall man called a pimp, who hung out on the corner and kept an eye on the girls. Sometimes he hit them, and Greta would hear screams and shouts. She'd cover her ears with her hands, trying to keep the sounds out.

Then Mom started bringing men home, men who gave her

money. Did that make her a hooker too? Greta didn't like to think about that. All she knew was that Mom would shut Hank and Greta out of the ugly room. They'd huddle together on the stairs that stank of urine, dodging the other residents of the hotel, those scary-looking weirdos Mom had warned Greta about, in those few times when she wasn't giggly and woozy from that stuff she was drinking.

One day Mom left. She said she was going to the store on the corner to get a bottle. But she never came back.

The manager of the hotel told Greta he was going to call social something to come and get the two children. But social something sounded like cops to Greta. She didn't want to go to jail or wherever the cops would take them. She packed what little they had in the nylon bag and they left. Now they lived on the streets and it was getting harder to find food and stay warm.

Hank, his stomach filled by the pepperoni pizza and the cookies Greta had stolen from the bakery, drowsed next to her, leaning on her shoulder. Greta put one arm around him as she savored the last bite of her chocolate chip cookie. Then she felt someone's eyes on her and looked quickly around, her senses honed by weeks of surviving on the urban landscape.

There he was, a man, staring at them across Union Square. She'd seen the man before, staring at them like this. He wore shapeless green coveralls, and stood hunched over the handle of a metal shopping cart. Inside the cart was a black plastic bag that clinked and clattered. Greta knew it was full of cans and bottles. The man had a black beard and a brown knit cap that didn't quite disguise his long black hair.

Greta didn't like the way he was always watching them. Then the man pushed his shopping cart toward them, the wheels squeaking. She jumped to her feet and shook Hank awake.

"Invisible time," she whispered.

That meant it was time for them to disappear into the shadows. She picked up the nylon bag and slung it over her shoulder, then took Hank's hand. The two children darted down the steps that led out of the square, across Geary Street, just as the green "walk" signal changed to a flashing amber "don't walk." As they angled to the left, Greta glanced back. The man in coveralls was following them, pushing his shopping cart into the crosswalk, ambling slowly as though he didn't care that the light had changed to red and the people in the going-home cars were honking at him.

Greta tugged Hank's arm and the two children rushed along Geary, dodging pedestrians. They turned right on Stockton, heading toward Market. Finally they pushed through a pair of big glass double doors and entered the first floor of the Virgin Megastore, sound pulsating around them.

They were in familiar territory now. The store was one of their favorite hangouts. It was brightly lit and full of loud music, where customers bought CDs, tapes, videos and books. It was open late and the children frequently spent the evening here, walking the aisles, riding the escalator up and down, and using the restroom on the third floor. Greta figured they'd lost the man with the shopping cart but even if they hadn't, he wouldn't be able to follow them in here.

"I'm sleepy," Hank told her on their fourth trip up the escalator. "Can we find a place to spend the night soon?"

Greta was tired, too, but she didn't like to admit it. Watching and moving all the time took its toll, but she was afraid to let her guard down. She wished they could find a spot somewhere in this bright warm store, but she knew that was a bad idea.

"Let's go to the bathroom first," she said. "Then we'll find a place."

They detoured to the third floor, past the videos and into the bookstore. The restrooms were located down a short hallway near the store's café. Greta watched Hank dart into the men's room, then pushed open the door marked with a woman's silhouette. Sometimes, if they didn't know the place, she'd take him with her into the women's side, where they'd barricade themselves into the larger stall usually reserved for handicapped people. But they'd been here before, and hadn't had any problems. Greta felt as safe here as she felt anywhere, which wasn't saying much.

When she came out of the restroom Hank was waiting for her, bouncing in time to the music that blared from the overhead speakers. Greta shifted the nylon bag from one shoulder to the other and they walked toward the café.

"You kids okay?"

The speaker was a young woman, wearing thick clunky shoes and black tights under a short black skirt. Above that she wore a tight black T-shirt with the store's name printed across her tiny round breasts. Her hair was cut short and dyed an odd bright pink. She had little gold rings arrayed up and down both ears, and a glittery jewel in her nose. Greta had seen her before, once working behind a cash register on the second floor and another time waiting tables in the store's café.

Hank stared at her, transfixed. Greta started looking around for the quickest and shortest way out.

"I've seen you before," the young woman said, talking quietly as though she were afraid they would bolt. "You come in and wander around for hours. Don't you have any place to stay?" When neither of the children answered, she continued, her voice low and seductive. "I'll bet you're hungry. Would you like something to eat? Come back to the café. I'll give you some gingerbread."

227

From the corner of her eye, Greta saw something move, a skinny form in a T-shirt that resolved itself into another store employee, this one a young man with white hair. Trap, she thought. They wouldn't be able to come in here again. If they ever got out.

"Invisible time," she hissed.

She grabbed Hank's arm and ran straight at the young woman, who held out her arms as though to catch them. Greta shoved her hard and the young woman fell back against a bin full of CDs. The young man who'd come to her assistance looked startled as the children darted past him. As they ran toward the down escalator, Greta heard voices behind her, all jumbled as the two sales clerks spoke together.

". . . Almost had them."

". . . Told you . . . bad idea. Shoulda called the cops."

"Poor little things . . . back tomorrow night . . . try again."

Won't be back, Greta told herself as she and Hank hurried down the escalator, heedless of bumping the customers who stood still on the moving stairs. Not safe anymore. Too bad. She hated to lose any shelter, however temporary.

It had started to rain while they were inside the store. Hand-in-hand, Greta and Hank rushed along the wet pavement, until they found themselves heading up Market Street, pushed along with a tide of people. At Sixth they crossed Market, wet and cold, and headed farther away from the bright holiday glitter of the city's main shopping area and into the dingy, neon-pierced blocks where the Tenderloin collided with the area South of Market. Here were lots of people sitting in doorways, bundled up against the rain. Music blared from bars. Hookers, some of them barely older than Greta, called to the passing cars.

These grown-ups scared Greta and she quickly detoured down a side street where it was much quieter. She found a wide doorway, recessed from the street. It looked like a good place to spend the night. She set the nylon bag down to use as a pillow. But then she spotted the man in green coveralls, back the way they'd come and moving toward them. He was close enough so that she was sure she could hear the clink and clatter of the bottles and cans in his garbage bag, the squeaking wheels of his shopping cart.

They kept moving, Hank stumbling along sleepily at her side. The nylon bag seemed as heavy as lead and Greta was so tired she thought she couldn't put another foot in front of her. Still she thought she could hear the shopping cart following them, squeaking and rattling as they fled through the wet curtain of rain.

Then she saw something flicker. Was she imagining it? No, it came from inside a big dark two-story building with broken glass windows. Greta crept closer and peered through the nearest window. But she couldn't see much, just something red and gold, glowing farther back in the dark building. She squinted and could just make out some figures nearby.

A fire, she thought. Just the word sounded like a sanctuary, warm and inviting. But there were people, and they could be bad people.

She heard a squeaking noise somewhere back the way they come, and made her choice. Quickly she boosted Hank up to the window, then followed him through, dragging the nylon bag with her. She held her finger to her mouth and tiptoed forward, trying not to make any noise as she moved closer to the fire.

She saw three grown-ups, two men and a woman. They'd spread big pieces of cardboard on the concrete floor of the empty warehouse, to cut the chill. On top of these the grown-ups had constructed their nests of sleeping bags and blankets. In the center they'd built a fire with whatever fuel they could find. Now it danced, red and gold, crackling and popping and hissing. The grown-ups talked in low voices, occasionally laughing as they drank from a bottle, its neck visible at the top of its brown paper bag wrapping. They passed it among themselves, and one of them leaned toward the fire to stir something that was bubbling in a big shiny kettle, something that smelled rich and savory like the soup Mom used to make.

Greta's foot encountered a piece of broken glass and sent it skittering across the concrete. The resulting tinkle heralded their arrival. The grown-ups grouped around the fire turned, seeking the source of the noise.

"Well, what have we here?" a voice boomed at them. It belonged to a big man with a white beard, bundled up in several layers of clothing, his eyes glittering in the firelight. "A couple of little angels with very dirty faces?"

"More like a couple of pups looking for a teat and a warm place to sleep." The woman who spoke had a hard face and hard eyes, but she reached for a tin mug and the ladle that protruded from the kettle on the fire. She spooned some of the hot liquid into the mug.

"Don't be feeding strays," complained the second man, a pale skinny fellow dressed in a dirty gray sweater. He reclined on a gray duffel bag and folded his arms in front of him.

"Don't tell me what to do," she snapped. Then she held out the mug and beckoned at the children. "Come here. It's vegetable soup. We made it ourselves and it's damned good, if I do say so myself."

Hank and Greta stared, mesmerized by the smell and the sight. Then they moved into the warm circle around the fire and sat at the foot of the woman's sleeping bag. Greta reached for the mug, felt the warmth on her hands, smelled the broth. Then she held the mug out to Hank. He drank noisily, hungrily. Yet he was careful to leave half the soup for his sister. He handed her the mug and wiped his mouth on his sleeve.

"You take care of him, don't you," the woman said, as Greta sipped warm soup from the mug. "Bet you do a good job, too. My name's Elva. This here's Wally." She pointed at the big man with the beard. "And this bag of bones is Jake."

Jake snorted, and sank further into the folds of his sleeping bag. He took a long pull from the bottle, then passed the libation to Wally. "What the hell you kids doing out here all by yourselves?"

"What are any of us doing out here?" Wally boomed, his voice echoing in the dark recesses of the warehouse. "Trying to stay warm, dry and fed." He tipped back the bottle and grinned at the two children across the glowing heat of the fire. "Look how skinny these little angels are. Stick with us, kids. We'll fatten you up."

Wary as she was after weeks of living on the streets, Greta was also tired. She felt exhaustion creep over her as the warmth of the soup and fire crept over her body. Already Hank was asleep, his little body burrowed into her side, like a puppy pillowed on its mother's belly.

"Look at 'em," Elva said. "Just babies. What you got in that bag, girl?"

"Clothes." Greta's tongue getting tangled up in the word.

"Not even a sleeping bag and winter coming on." Elva shook her head. She pulled a raggedy square of cloth that looked like a piece of an old blanket from the depths of her sleeping bag. Then she scooted forward and used it to cover Hank, fussing with the edge as she tucked it around his neck, just the way Mom used to. "Where's your folks?"

"Gone," Greta said, and the word seemed to echo around the warehouse.

Elva frowned and looked at her companions. "All alone? How long you been out here, girl?"

Greta found that she didn't have strength enough to answer. She felt all her caution fall to the onslaught of sleep.

"We can't be baby-sitting a couple of kids."

Greta's eyes were shut, but she identified the voice. It belonged to Jake, the skinny one.

"No one's asking you to look after 'em. They can go with me."

That was Elva, the woman. Greta opened her eyes just a little bit. It was morning, cold gray light filtering into the warehouse. The fire was out, cold gray ashes swirling along the concrete floor. Greta felt warm, though. The children were tucked into Elva's sleeping bag. Hank was next to Greta, curled up in a ball and still asleep.

"Just slow you down," Jake growled as he rolled up his sleeping bag. "Make you a target for the cops. They don't even look like they're yours."

"What the hell do you know?" Elva scowled at him. "All anybody's gonna see is some poor homeless woman with a couple of kids she can't feed. Which ain't far from the truth. With Christmas coming on, people feel generous and guilty. I'll just park the three of us out in front of San Francisco Centre where all those rich people ride that fancy curved escalator up to Nordstrom. You just see how many handouts I get. Take my word, these kids'll be worth their weight in greenbacks."

"More trouble than they're worth, you ask me," Jake grumbled as he tied his sleeping bag with rope.

"Nobody asked you," Elva shot back.

"Now, friends, friends. Let's not come blows, whether with words or fists." That was Wally, the big guy with the beard. "I agree with Elva. We should care for these little angels. I'm sure we'll be handsomely rewarded. Yes, indeed."

Wally laughed. He was pretending to be nice, Greta decided, but he wasn't. She didn't like the way his eyes glittered when he looked at her and Hank. She abandoned all pretense of sleep and sat up. The nylon bag was no longer beside her, but next to Elva, who had rummaged through its contents. Greta snatched up the picture of Mom and hugged the frame to her chest.

"That your mama?" Elva asked. "She was real pretty." The woman reached over and shook Hank awake. "Let's put another layer of clothes on you, 'cause it's cold out there this morning."

The three grown-ups stashed their sleeping bags in a small room in the bowels of the abandoned warehouse and set out with the two children. In the bleak daylight the South of Market neighborhood didn't look as scary as it had last night, just dirty and down at heels.

Jake set off on his own, heading up Mission Street, but Wally stayed with Elva and the children until they reached Market. Then he bid them an elaborate and flowery farewell, lingering until Elva told him to get the hell on with it. He bowed, crossed the street, and headed for the Tenderloin.

Then Elva took Hank and Greta another block down Market and did just what she'd said she'd do. She took a position in front of the San Francisco Centre and started cadging handouts from well-heeled shoppers. Soon she had enough money to send the children across Market to the fast-food burger place. Hank ate two cheeseburgers and a big order of French fries all by himself.

"I like Elva," he declared, wiping ketchup from his mouth.

He doesn't know things the way I do, Greta thought. He's just a baby, not experienced like me. I'm not so sure but what we're better off on our own.

She brooded as she finished her hamburger. Then she cleared off the table and stepped up to the counter to buy another one, for Elva.

But even if Greta had her doubts about staying with the trio from the warehouse, it was easy to slip into the routine, the next day and the day after. They worked the streets with Elva during the day, going from store to store, hotel to hotel, then met Jake and Wally back at the warehouse. Wally found a sleeping bag for the two children to share, and each day the three grown-ups managed to find enough food to put into the kettle. It was so easy to feel comfortable and safe, huddled in the warm circle of the fire on the warehouse's concrete floor. In the morning they'd roll up their sleeping bags and stash their gear in the little room, then head out for a day on the streets.

The two children had been staying at the warehouse for a couple of weeks when Greta saw Wally talking with the tall man from the Tenderloin, the pimp who had all those hookers working for him. She and Hank and Elva were working the Geary Theatre that day. It was a natural, Elva told them. Theatre patrons left the comfortable confines where they'd seen a seasonal matinee of *A Christmas Carol*, and stepped onto the dirty city streets and came face-to-face with a couple of contemporary urchins.

"Guilt and generosity," Elva said confidently. "It'll do it every time."

After the matinee Elva led them down Taylor toward Market Street, through the Tenderloin, where Greta saw Wally. He spotted the children and waved. Why was Wally talking to that awful pimp man? Why did Wally's eyes glitter like that, above his white beard? She didn't like it. Especially since Wally came back to the warehouse that night with a big bottle of brandy, evidently the kind Jake and Elva liked a lot, because they drank the whole bottle that night, laughing loudly and acting silly, so drunk they finally passed out and Greta had to finish making dinner under Wally's watchful eyes.

When she woke up the next morning, her head pillowed on the nylon bag, Jake and Elva were still asleep, a couple of lumps in their sleeping bags, snoring like they were sawing logs.

But Wally was gone. So was Hank.

Greta kicked her way out of the sleeping bag and put on her shoes. "Hank?" she called. There was no answer. She darted around the bottom floor of the warehouse, looking for her brother, getting more frantic as she looked in all the shadowy places.

On her third circuit she encountered Wally, who was making his way back into the warehouse with a bag and a large container that smelled like coffee. "What's the matter, little angel?" he asked jovially.

"Hank's gone," she cried.

"I'm sure he's just wandered off." Wally waggled the bag at her. "Doughnuts, little angel. Jelly doughnuts and chocolate bars. I know you like chocolate. Want one?"

"He wouldn't wander off," Greta said stubbornly. "He knows he's supposed to stick close to me."

Greta ran back to where Jake and Elva still lay snoring. She shook Elva but the woman wouldn't wake up.

"Oh, I wouldn't bother," Wally said, placing a heavy hand on her shoulder. "When those two get a snootful of brandy it would take an earthquake to wake them. Maybe two earthquakes. Have a doughnut. We want to fatten you up."

Fatten me up for what? Greta glared at him. "I don't want a doughnut. I have to look for Hank."

"Have you looked on the second floor? Maybe he went exploring up there."

"How would he get there?" Greta knew there was another floor above this one but she hadn't seen any stairs or an elevator, not that an elevator would work in this place.

"Why, there's some stairs down at the other end, next to what used to be the elevator shaft." Wally laughed and pointed into the dark bowels of the warehouse. "Wait, I'll come with you."

Greta ran ahead, frantic with worry about Hank. She found the stairs and clambered up them, calling for her brother. She heard Wally behind her, chuckling to himself as he climbed the stairs.

Hank wasn't on the second floor of the warehouse. Or if he was, he wasn't answering her. Greta felt tears prickling behind her eyes as she searched the big empty space, skirting the hole near the stairs, where Wally said there used to be an elevator.

"Why, look at this," Wally said. She looked in the direction he was pointing. There was a doorway, open, with blackness beyond. "There's rooms back there. Maybe that's where your brother's gone."

She didn't trust the bearded man, but she had to find Hank. She walked toward the doorway and peered into the dimly-lit chamber, her eyes adjusting, picking out shapes. This part of the warehouse had been used as offices, about a quarter of the floor carved up into cubicles by partitions. There was a door on the far side next to a dirty window.

"Hank?" she called, her voice echoing against the walls.

Was that a voice she heard, just a whimper? Maybe he had wandered in here and gotten hurt or something. She moved into the divided-up room, heard Wally step in after her, then whirled in alarm as she heard the door shut. Wally laughed. A few seconds later this portion of the room was brightened by the circular glow from a big flashlight.

In that instant she saw Hank. He was under an old metal desk, his hands tied to one of the legs with a length of rope. He'd been crying, but he stopped when he saw Greta.

She ran to Hank and scrabbled at the rope with her fingers. It wasn't tied very well. If she had enough time, she could get it loose. But did she have enough time?

She turned and shouted at Wally. "What have you done to him?"

Wally laughed, a nasty sound. "Caught me a pair of plump little partridges, that's what. You and him both."

"What are you talking about?" Greta demanded.

"Been talking to a man. The kind of man who'll pay good money for a couple of fat little angels like you. Oh, yes. The kind that likes little boys will have a good time with your little brother. Then there's the kind that likes sweet little virgins like you."

Wally shifted the flashlight from his right hand to his left. Greta saw his right hand go into his pocket and pulled out a handful of greenbacks. "This is just seed money. I get the rest when I deliver the goods, when the man comes through that fire escape door in a few minutes."

A few minutes. That's all the time she had. Wally was between her and the door. Greta squatted and tugged at the rope securing Hank's hands, her fingers working the knot. There, it was loosening. Just a little bit more, that's all she needed.

"Look at him," she cried, making her voice teary. "You got it so tight it's cutting his hands. That's why he's been crying."

Hank didn't need to be told twice. He started to wail. Greta joined in, still fumbling with the rope.

237

"Shut up, both of you," Wally said, shoving the money back into his pocket. "Shut up, I tell you."

Wally walked to the desk and knelt, setting the flashlight aside so he could adjust the rope. Quick as lightening Greta scooped it up and brought it down hard on Wally's head. He bellowed and grabbed for her as he tried to get to his feet. She slithered from his grasp, then hit him again and he went down. She hit him a third time and he moaned. Then she turned to Hank and helped her little brother pull free of his bonds.

She seized her brother's arm and tugged him toward the door. When they reached it, she jerked it open and they ran for the stairwell. Hank had just reached the top step when Greta was caught from behind. Wally was cursing in her ear as he lifted her off the floor. She wriggled in his arms, almost gagging at the smell of him, and sank her teeth into one of the hands that held her. He screamed as she tasted blood. He dropped her.

She regained her balance and turned to face him as he came at her again, aiming her fist at the crotch of his baggy pants, at the place Mom said it would hurt if you hit a man. He screamed again when she hit him, falling backwards. But he didn't fall onto the floor. He kept going back, and down, into the open elevator shaft.

"He went splat," Hank said when she found him at the bottom of the stairwell.

"Good. I hope he broke his damn neck."

Greta looked dispassionately at the motionless body lying on top of the rusted metal at the bottom of the elevator shaft, about three feet below the first floor of the warehouse. Blood trickled from his mouth. When he didn't move, she climbed down and reached into his pocket, pulling out the folded money he'd been showing off. He wouldn't be needing it anymore.

Greta shoved the money into her own pocket, climbed out of the shaft and took Hank's arm. They ran through the warehouse, back to where Jake and Elva were still sleeping it off next to the gray ashes of the fire. Greta scooped up the bag of doughnuts and zipped them inside the brown nylon bag. No sense letting food go to waste.

"Where we going now?" Hank asked.

She slung the bag over her shoulder and headed for the street. "Invisible time."